STEEL

DELTA FORCE GUARDIANS

SUSIE MCIVER

DELTA FORCE GUARDIANS
BOOK TWO

STEEL

AUTHOR
SUSIE MCIVER

Copyright © 2024 by Susie McIver

All rights reserved.

No part of this publication may be reproduced, distributed, or transmitted in

any form or by any means, including photocopying, recording, or other electronic or mechanical

methods, without the prior written permission of the publisher, except as permitted by U.S.

copyright law. For permission request, contact Susie McIver susie.mciver@yahoo.com

The story all names, characters, and incidents portrayed in this production

Are fictitious. No identification with actual persons (living or deceased),

places, buildings, and products is intended or should be inferred.

Cover by- Maria at Steamy Designs

Cover photo by- Wander Aguiar photography

Model-Zack B

❀ Created with Vellum

1

STEEL

"Spike!" I hollered, trying to locate my dog. "Spike, you've got five minutes to get back home before I come after you." This was unusual behavior for Spike; he typically stayed close to home. Worried, I began to search around the house to see if he might be sleeping somewhere. After all, he was getting up there in dog years, equivalent to seventy in human years. My heart raced with fear that he might be injured. I decided to head to the swimming hole to check if he was there.

I heard a scream as I walked uphill to the swimming hole. A woman in a wheelchair came barreling down the hill, and I had a sinking feeling she was about to end up in the cold water. I ran toward her, and just as I expected, she splashed into the water, letting out another scream. I ran to where she was, quickly righted her wheelchair, and helped her out of the water. She was trembling, so I took off my shirt and wrapped it around her for warmth.

It was then that I recognized her as the niece of the Randal sisters. I remembered her as a tall, skinny girl with braces, but she had changed considerably. She no longer had braces, and the closer I looked, the more I could see she was no longer skinny; she had plenty of curves. I wondered why she was in a wheelchair. She was still tall, and gazing at her, I saw she was as beautiful as she always had been. I remembered her mom was Spanish, so she had all that dark hair and big brown eyes.

Her expression seemed ready to unleash fury, and I assumed her anger was directed at one of her aunts, who, at this moment, was running down the hill, yelling she was sorry. I just knew she was going to come sliding into us. "They are going to kill me if I stay here any longer," Charlie muttered to herself. "I desperately need to return to my own home. I don't care what Dad says. My aunts are too clumsy to help me. I told my father, but would he listen to me? No, he said my aunts begged him to take care of me while I healed from my wounds. I've had enough."

That's when Miss Molly showed up. "I'm so sorry, dear. Your large dog startled me, and I accidentally bumped into your wheelchair. That's why I always ask that you sit in one of the chairs on the porch. I've been so concerned about this hill and the swimming hole."

"Aunt Molly, I think it's time I went home. I'm too much work for you and Aunt Hillary."

"Nonsense, Levi, can you please push Charlotte Primrose back up the hill to our house?"

I noticed that mentioning her middle name caused her to shudder. If I remember correctly, she has always hated her middle name. I remembered her telling me once that her aunts named her. The house was a very large Victorian. Charlie suddenly realized I was there and heard her talking to herself.

She looked down at my shirt wrapped around her. She looked back at me, "Levi, I'm sorry for ignoring you. Thank you for saving me. I doubt I could have crawled from the swimming hole alone. It must have shocked you when you realized you had saved the life of that buck-toothed, long-legged, stringy-haired witch. Or wait, I believe what you said was bitch."

"Now Charlotte, Levi was a child when he said that, and if I remember right, you let him have it with a swift kick in his shins for saying that to you," Aunt Molly said. I watched as Charlie shook her head; I stopped pushing and walked around to examine her. She was bleeding from a spot on her forehead. "I'm sorry I was a stupid jerk when I was sixteen. I was so upset when that ball hit me in the face because my dog Rover had just died. I know you can never forgive me; it's obvious you haven't forgotten it if you remember it word for word."

"I promise I went up to tell you how sorry I was, but you had already left and never returned. I wrote you a letter; I gave it to Miss Hilary to mail to you."

"Well, that was your first mistake. Aunt Hilary can never remember anything. Forget about it."

"Let me look at you. You must have hit your head; it's bleeding."

"I hit a bush before going into the water. It'll be fine. I just need to get back to the house and take a warm bath."

"Can you walk at all?"

"Yes, I can walk; it's just still painful. I need to go home, where I have all my equipment to help me. I have to push myself, and that's hard to do with my aunts trying to make me sit down all the time. They watch me like I'm a newborn baby. I'll call my father and have him come and get me."

"I can help you. I have nothing going on right now," I noticed her frown.

"You don't have a job?" She asked with those beautiful brows raised.

"Remember, dear, I told you about the boys here who left the Marines and started their own security business," Aunt Hillary said.

"We actually have a high-security business and travel worldwide for rescue missions," I added, feeling compelled to explain our work to her.

"That must be a rewarding job. Mine felt rewarding before the accident. Now I'm happy if I can get to the bathroom alone. I'm sorry; it's just that I get so frustrated that my recovery is taking so long."

"When was your accident?" I asked.

"Six months ago. An eighteen-wheeler hit me, and it wasn't an accident; the driver wanted me dead. He almost succeeded, but there was a police car at the red light next to me. The police officer had to kill the driver because he was coming at me with a gun in his hand. He was angry because his brother was murdered in prison, and he blamed me."

"Wow, an eighteen-wheeler? You're lucky to be alive. I have all the equipment you'll need at my place. I'll come and pick you up in the morning. What time should I be here?" I could tell she didn't want me helping her, so I waited patiently for an answer. "Seven in the morning if that's good for you."

"Seven is perfect; I'll pick you up." I pushed her into the house, "Where's your room?"

"The parlor is my room while I'm recovering." I pushed her to the bathroom and started her bathwater. "That's okay, I can do that myself," she said, but I had already started the water. "Jeez, why do people think I need everything done for me," Charlie whispered, but I heard.

"It's no trouble."

"Charlotte Primrose, what happened to you?" Miss Hilary exclaimed.

"I went swimming. Thank you, Levi; I'll see you in the morning."

I looked up Charlie's accident on the computer when I got home. Spike walked into my office, and I scolded him for running off. What I saw on the screen was unreal. There was nothing left of her car; it was a miracle she survived. It was no wonder her recovery was taking so long.

Curious, I decided to do some more research on her. She had attended The University of Texas in Austin, her hometown. Her father was an inventor, and her mother was a librarian. I couldn't help but wonder how she became a Homicide Detective.

"What are you doing?" my sister Jaz asked, standing behind me. "Hey, that's Charlie? I remember her; she was my age. Why are you investigating her?"

"I'm not investigating her; she's at her aunt's recovering from an injury. I'm going to help her to walk again." Come over here, and I'll show you her accident," I handed her boys some paper to color on and some crayons I kept there for them. Jaz grabbed a chair and pulled it up next to me.

"She can't walk?"

"I told you she was injured. She says she can walk, but it's still painful. She's trying to get her muscles stronger, at least that's what I'm thinking. I'll pick her up in the mornings and take her back after a few hours."

"Wow, that's horrible, and she's still alive; my goodness, that must have been a nightmare. Why is she at her aunt's house?"

"Because her father and aunts thought it was a good idea for them to care for her. Hell, she would be better off alone.

At least I can help her a few hours a day until I return to work."

"How much longer are you going to be off?"

"Maybe a month. What are you and these two rascals doing?" "We're taking a walk. We thought we would ask you to accompany us; we're going to Bailey's."

"Sure, let's go. Maybe we'll be invited for dinner. Come, Spike," we walked out on the porch, and Mertle lay there. She was still angry at me for getting her fixed. It took me forever to give her pups away with the last litter. Come on, Mertle, you can visit your son at Bailey and Viper's house."

2

CHARLIE

I LONGED TO FIND A HIDDEN PLACE TO ESCAPE THE SITUATION I was now in. I submerged myself beneath the water in the bathtub, contemplating how long I could remain concealed while my aunts persistently knocked on the door. The danger I had just narrowly avoided was terrifying. I had every intention of calling my mother and venting my frustration.

I am so embarrassed that Levi had to save me. I was grateful he was there, or I would have had to float until my aunts found help. And Levi's so handsome. He's always been attractive, but now he was a grown man who smelled so good.

I had a crush on him when I was thirteen, but now I needed to ensure he never discovered my feelings. I believed I could manage it, especially knowing his Delta Force code name was 'Steel.' The name suited him perfectly.

After my aunts helped me out of the tub, I crawled into bed, and as soon as they left my room, I called my mother.

"Hello, darling. How's everything going?" she greeted.

"Mama, if Dad doesn't show up in two days, I'm leaving

on my own. I had a near-death experience today because Aunt Molly accidentally pushed my wheelchair, and I went flying down the mountain and I fell into that freezing swimming hole. I could have exacerbated my injuries and had irreparable damage or died."

"Now honey, don't you think you might be exaggerating a little? I'm sure they're doing their best; I bet Aunt Molly feels terrible about what happened. I hope you didn't yell at her."

I took a deep breath and counted to ten. "Mama, have I ever yelled at anyone that you know of? Did you ever get a letter for me from Levi Peterson years ago?"

"We did, but we thought you were too young to receive mail from boys. I was hoping you didn't find out about that."

"Mom, it was an apology letter because he yelled at me."

"We found that out after we opened it, and by then, it was too late to give it to you since it had already been opened."

"So you read a letter meant for me and then persuaded me to come here and let my bumbling aunts take care of me. You even made me feel guilty for not wanting to come here. What the hell is going on? I'm serious; tell me what Dad and the aunts have cooked up?"

"I don't know what you're talking about. Oh, I have to go. Goodbye, honey," she abruptly hung up. I'm going to figure out what those three are plotting, even if it's the last thing I do.

My aunts had raised my father after their parents passed away. He said Molly took care of him before they even died. There was a twenty-year age gap between my father and his sisters because he had been a surprise addition to the family. Grandma was fifty-six when she gave birth to him.

Aunt Hilary said it was the talk of the mountain when he was born.

My father went to college in Texas, where he met my mom, and decided never to leave Texas. My uncle on my mother's side was a homicide detective, and I decided that was what I wanted to be.

Over the years, I had kept up with the people on the mountain, primarily Levi Peterson. I had refused to return because he was so mean the last time I was here. I came back a few times while he was in the service. I even saw him at the little grocery store when I visited for a few days, and I snuck out so he couldn't see me. I left the mountain before I saw him again.

He had sent me an apology letter, and I had carried around my anger all these years. He had been in pain due to his dog's death and had lashed out at me. He felt remorse almost immediately afterward. I remembered his dog, who was always by his side. I couldn't bear the thought of losing my own dog, Sara.

Since my accident, she has been my constant companion. Sara, a Bernese mountain dog and a golden retriever mix, was large but incredibly friendly. I can still see her running down the mountain after my wheelchair. I looked around, and there she was, sleeping on the rug.

"Would you like dinner now?" Aunt Hillary asked, peeking her head around the door.

"Aunt Hillary, what made you and my Dad decide to have me come here?"

"We wanted to ensure you were well taken care of, rather than having a stranger take care of you," Aunt Hillary said.

"So, did my father call you and ask if you could care for me? It has to be hard on you and Aunt Molly, having me underfoot all the time, waiting on me, day and night."

"No, dear, not at all. We enjoy your company. Let's talk about what you'll wear when Steel picks you up in the morning?" Aunt Hilary said, pushing me into the dining room.

"You call him Steel? I thought his team called him Steel?"

"No, everyone here calls him Steel except Molly and his aunts. Sometimes, other family members will call him Levi. But you have to admit, he looks like he's all Steel.

"Aunt Hilary," I exclaimed in disbelief.

"I might be getting close to eighty, but I can recognize a handsome man when I see one. All of those Peterson men are attractive. Actually, most of the men around here are handsome. I guess you heard that Cole Reed wasn't dead; he was locked up in an Iranian prison. Now, he's married to Bailey Peterson. Bailey never knew she had any family until Cole came into her life. Now she has lots of family members."

"That's a miracle that he was alive."

Hillary scooted closer to me. "Don't get me started on gossiping. There is so much happening on this mountain. You wouldn't believe what you can learn sitting in the doctor's office."

"What are you talking about?" Aunt Molly asked.

"I was telling Charlie about Cole Reed and his wife, Bailey."

"We also learned Izzy is a Peterson and Bailey's sister. So much has happened it will take us weeks to catch you up on everything. Ryan Reed is with Carly Harlow. I remember seeing her hiding in the woods with her dog. She had to hide whenever that mean Jim Harlow would get drunk or he would beat her. Yes, a lot has happened since we were young girls."

"Did either of you ever fall in love?"

"Molly fell deeply in love when she was eighteen. Joesph Walsh was so handsome, and he loved Molly profoundly. It was almost embarrassing being around them."

"What happened to him?"

"He ended up marrying someone else. His father was involved in illegal money laundering at the bank, and the father of the woman who Joseph married threatened to expose Mr. Walsh to the authorities if Joseph didn't marry his daughter. It was a terrible ordeal, filled with a million tears."

Molly wiped a tear away. "Joseph always came to see me while I was away at college; he explained everything to me. He told me he would love me forever, and I knew I couldn't love anyone else. So, I went to school and learned everything about the banking business. After graduating, I set out to ruin Joseph's father and his wife's father. I succeeded in banking, but when I saw Joesph with his son, I stopped trying to destroy them. I didn't want to be like those men. Plus, I had your Dad to raise; he came first in my life.

"I'm so sorry, Auntie. That must have been an incredibly difficult time for you, so much that it affected the rest of your life."

"I have a secret," Aunt Molly blurted out.

"No, you do not, Molly. Look at me. There's no secret. This isn't about you anymore; it's about others now," I couldn't believe that my Aunt Hilary appeared ready to sew my Aunt Molly's lips together. What in the world is the secret?

They both sat up straight in their chairs, not uttering a word. I looked at one and then the other. "You must be joking; you can't just stop there. I have to know the secret."

"There is no secret," Molly confessed. "Sometimes I say

that just to see how Hilary will react, and she always reacts the same way. She gets angry, thinking I'm going to reveal a secret."

I knew my aunts were keeping a secret, but I didn't push it further because I saw the distress it caused Hilary. But whatever the secret was, it was big, and I didn't know if I wanted to learn what it was.

This was the first time I thought of my aunts as real women who loved someone so much that it could destroy their lives for others. Damn, am I going to cry? We continued to eat, and I decided to lighten it up a little. "So, what should I wear for my workout with your handsome neighbor?"

"Oh, he is so cute with those dreamy silver eyes and all those muscles," Hilary said. "You should wear those tight leggings with that violet tank top. He'll soon realize that you're also quite fit but in a sexy curvy way."

"Auntie, are you trying to embarrass me?"

"No, dear, I'm just telling the truth. You should wear your hair in a braid down your back; it's beautiful however you wear it. I'm so happy you are getting this help from Steel. If anyone can make you one hundred percent better, he can. You'll be running in these hills in no time," My aunt looked at me. "Do you miss Texas? Did you have someone special there?"

"I miss Texas a little, and no, I don't have anyone special. Once, I thought I did, but he turned out to be a bastard, so nope, no one." If I had looked at my aunts, I would have seen the excitement in their eyes upon hearing this news.

3
STEEL

I arrived at Molly's door promptly at six-forty-five, and Molly answered. "Good morning, Levi. How can I assist you today?"

"Oh dear, please come in; I forgot you were picking up Charlie," Molly said as she turned to get Charlie, and I couldn't help the anticipation building inside me.

Then Charlie was there. "Here I am, ready to start my workout," I turned my head, and she stood with her crutches. My heart did something, and I shut it down before it could do anything else.

"Great, are you comfortable with those?" I asked, gesturing towards her crutches.

"Yes, I am. I haven't tried walking outside with them, and I thought if I'm going to give it a shot, why not with you nearby to catch me if I stumble?" Charlie replied.

"Yes," she confirmed.

"How about I carry you to my truck? That way, your first experience outside with the crutches won't involve going downhill."

"I'll carry your crutches to the truck while Levi carries you," Molly said.

I held Charlie in my arms, holding her perhaps a tad closer than necessary, and gently placed her in the truck. Her scent filled my senses.

"So, how mobile are you? I want to make sure you don't overexert yourself," I inquired.

"I'm not as mobile as I want to be, but the doctors all said I'd never walk again. So, I'm happy to say I showed them."

"Can you stand on your own at all?" I asked.

"Yes, but not for a long period of time. I need to strengthen my legs. It's been five months since they told me I couldn't walk."

"You are doing an amazing job," I assured her.

"I looked into your accident, and it was truly horrific."

"Yes, it was, but it wasn't an accident. The man wanted me dead. He blamed me for his brother dying in prison because I was the arresting officer, and he was determined to kill me."

"They all think I'm dead."

"Because when I left the scene in the ambulance, I was declared dead. But I shocked the hell out of the EMTs when I opened my eyes. It was reported that I had died, and my uncle kept it that way."

"I'm sorry you had to go through all of that pain. So why are you staying here with your aunts and not somewhere more hidden?"

"That's something my father and aunts planned; I have no idea why they wanted me here."

"How did you get here?"

"My dad flew me here."

"Your dad owns a plane?" I asked, a little surprised.

"Yes, he's a successful entrepreneur, inventing various kitchen gadgets and other things. He seems to have a knack for knowing what people want."

As we pulled into my long driveway, Mertle and Spike, my dogs, were waiting for me. As soon as we stopped, another dog ran up to us. "I wonder whose dog this is," I said, opening Charlie's door.

"Sara, what are you doing here? She must have followed us," Charlie said, turning toward me. "This is Sara, and she's my dog."

"She's welcome here. What kind of dog is she?"

"She's a Bernese and Golden Retriever mix."

"She's beautiful."

"So are yours."

"Shall we get started," I said, picking her up and carrying her inside.

"I need to use my crutches. How will I learn if you carry me everywhere?"

I smiled as I walked inside and went straight to my home gym.

"Wow! This place is amazing." Charlie said.

"Yeah, my team and I work out every day. Most of them get here at four or five in the morning."

"I hope I'm not interrupting any of their workouts."

"No, you're not. They're finished for the day. Would you like to start on the parallel bars?"

"Umm, okay."

"I'll be right behind you; I won't let you fall," I sat her down and let her place her hands on the bars.

"You don't have to stand so close. As long as you are in the room, it's fine. I'm not afraid I'll fall. I'll go real slow."

"Okay, I'll be ten feet away at the weights. Just say my name if you need help."

"Thank you."

Watching her cautiously navigate the bars, I recognized what she required to progress. She might not like it, but it was necessary. I approached her. "Your legs need to be massaged to improve circulation. I'm surprised they didn't tell you that before releasing you from the hospital."

"It's hard for me to have them massaged because they are still so tender."

"I'll be gentle. Let's give it a try."

"Alright." I carried her to the gym table, intending to apply some oil. "I need to rub oil on your legs. Can I give you something of my sisters to wear?"

"No. You can massage them with oil tomorrow," Charlie said, frowning.

"Alright, but starting tomorrow, we will rub your legs down first." I began gently massaging her legs, surprised she was letting me do this. "Can you turn onto your stomach?"

"I have a proposal for you. A simple yes or no will do. How about staying here? You'll have someone close to assist you. I don't think your aunts can take care of you. They're welcome to visit as often as they'd like, but let's be realistic; if you were to fall, they'd need to call for help," I spoke fast, before she could butt into my speech.

"I know, but I hate to hurt their feelings; otherwise, I'd consider your offer." It was clear she was just being polite. There was no way she would stay. Hmm, I might just fix it, so she had to accept.

"When I carried her inside, the Randal sisters were there to greet us. I placed Charlie in a chair and then fetched her wheelchair from her room. All three of them watched me closely. "I thought you might want your wheelchair. If you need anything, don't hesitate to call me," I said, glancing at Charlie's aunts and smiling. "I offered Charlie the option to stay at my home for better assistance, but she didn't want to offend you," I said, noting their exchanged glances.

"I think that will be a wonderful idea," Hilary exclaimed. "Let me pack her things; if we forget anything, we'll bring it over to you."

"But you wanted me here so you could care for me," Charlie protested.

"Yes, but Steel is better equipped for that than we are, Molly interjected. "I packed all of your bathroom items. We'll visit you every day. Do you need anything else?"

I had to bite my jaw to keep from smiling at the look on Charlie's face. I realized this had been easier than I thought. I picked her up and carried her back out to the truck, then retrieved her wheelchair while the aunts carried out her bags.

"Wait, just a moment. If I do not stay here, I'm going home. I came here because you begged for me to come here. I'll call my Uncle to pick me up. I can't live in a man's house I barely know," Charlie declared.

"You know me," I asserted.

"No, I don't. I was a child the last time I saw you, and that wasn't a pleasant memory in my life. Thank you for the offer, but I can't accept."

"Be honest with me; can anyone at your home provide as much help as I can?"

"That's not what this is about..." Charlie began, but I knew I had to convince her to stay. I don't know why I just know I did.

"Do you want to regain the ability to move freely around this area? If so, stay with me, and let me assist you. There are always people at my house. You can trust me; I won't do anything other than help you to walk again."

"Okay, but only for a month, and my aunts have to visit me daily."

"We'll be there tomorrow, and I'll bring anything left behind, Aunt Molly said, smiling."

I wanted to get the hell out of there before Charlie changed her mind. So, I backed the vehicle up and left.

4

CHARLIE

How did this happen? Here I am, sitting in Levi's house while he prepares lunch for us.

"Hello, I remember you. Charlie, right?" I turned my head and smiled at the woman and two little boys. "Yes. Jaz, I remember you too, but who are these two?" I said, looking down at the cute little toddlers.

"These are my boys, Caleb and Cruise. So, how are you doing? I heard about your accident. That must have been a nightmare for you."

"Yes, it was. Levi is going to help me get my legs stronger so I can walk again."

"That's wonderful news. If anyone can do it, it's Steel," I watched as she reached down and handed the boys some carrot sticks.

"Your boys are beautiful; they must bring you a lot of joy," I said, watching them sit quietly and eat their snacks. I hoped to have my own kids someday, but my doctor said that might not happen because of all the damage I sustained.

"Are you okay?" Levi asked. That's when I realized my eyes were welling up. I quickly blinked away the tears.

"Yes, I'm fine, thank you," I said as he placed a hamburger in front of me. Then he gave one to Jaz, the boys sat down and started eating their hamburgers. Before I knew it, they were finished and eating their fries.

Levi sat down and placed two yogurts in front of the boys. They started eating them along with their fries. I couldn't help but laugh as they dipped their fries into their yogurt.

"You're so lucky to have these little guys. They are so precious."

"Thank you. I was truly blessed when my boys were born. Keeping up with them is a challenge. So I bring them here, and Steel helps me; they don't try anything with him around. All he has to do is look at them, and they sit still."

I chuckled. "I bet they're full of energy. Do you live close by?"

Jaz nodded, "I live just down the street from here. Our entire family lives close by. Our parents retired to Miami, but they're moving back."

"It's so nice that you can visit your brother whenever you want. I grew up with my cousin Marcus. He's an FBI special agent, and he's been undercover for two years, so I hardly ever get to see him. There were no other kids in our family."

"I imagine that was lonely for you," Jaz said.

"No, it wasn't, I wasn't used to having other kids around so it was okay. My dad was like having kids around, and I was never lonely. He was always busy inventing things and wanted me involved in his projects."

"How cool. Did you invent anything yourself?"

"Yeah, I invented a few things. Once you start, you keep trying new things."

"What did you invent?"

"Just some small items to help you stack stuff in the kitchen or bathroom."

"Oh my goodness, did you invent Stackable No Space?"

"Yeah, that was one of my inventions. I invented that in college because I had no space for anything."

"I have that in my kitchen and bathroom. My house is super small, so I need all the space-saving solutions I can get."

"I'm glad you find them useful. I also use the stackable on my dresser for small items, so my dresser isn't cluttered; I'm a collector of little things, so my dresser fills up fast," I said, glancing at Levi, who had been listening to our conversation.

"So, you're not just a homicide detective but also an entrepreneur?" Levi asked, looking at me.

"Yeah, it's a bit of a habit. I guess I take after my father," I realized I hadn't noticed the sparkles in his eyes before. Staying here with Levi was proving to be a tempting proposition, and I was no longer angry at him for his past behavior. Since I now knew how horrible a day he was having that day. His poor dog had died. He must have been heartbroken.

"How about if we do some more workouts this evening? That way, you won't overexert yourself."

"Sure, that sounds good. Can I use the gym anytime to work on the parallel bars?"

"Of course, as long as you don't push yourself too hard."

"I'm going to make sure Sara isn't getting into trouble. She's used to being in a fenced yard. I'm sure she's having a blast right now. If it's okay with you, I'll bring her inside for a while."

"Let me get her for you, or would you prefer to sit on the

porch?" Levi asked, I knew he was trying to make me feel at home.

"I would love that, thank you."

"I should get these two little guys home before they fall asleep; it's nap time," Jaz said, gathering her boys.

I got my crutches, went to the front porch, and stopped. Sara and a German shepherd were stuck together. I hadn't even had her spayed yet.

Steel glanced at the dogs for a second. "Damn it, Spike, I'm going to have to keep you penned up. I didn't want to, but it has to be done," Levi said before turning to look at me. Jaz giggled as she walked off the porch.

"I honestly don't know what to say," Levi remarked, but I could see the laughter in his eyes.

"There really isn't a lot to say. Dogs are naturally horny, right?" I said, with a chuckle.

"Well, I know Spike is," Both of us laughed, and I realized I hadn't laughed much in the last few years. Being a homicide detective didn't leave much room for laughter.

"Sam, where the heck are you? I'm going to have to restrict your freedom," a beautiful woman said, looking our way. Then Levi glanced at the dogs again.

"Bailey, here he is."

The woman I now knew as Bailey smiled until she saw the dogs and then screamed. "Who taught him this stuff? Sam, you are a naughty dog. Whose dog is the other one? This is so bad."

"Bailey, this is Charlie. The naughty dog belongs to her, and I don't think she appreciates you calling her dog that."

"I did not call her dog that; you did. If I did, I'm sorry, but I said Sam was naughty. I'm just in shock at seeing my dog doing this. Can we please walk on the other side of the house? I can't bear to look at them. I'll never look at Sam the same way. I'm happy to meet you, Charlie."

"Don't worry about it, Bailey; I don't like looking at them either. So if Sam is with Sara, where is Spike?" I asked, looking at Levi.

"Spike," he yelled, walking away. I wondered if I could stand; he looked concerned, and my heart went out to him. I wanted to help him find Spike because I remembered he was concerned about Spike getting older.

"Come on, boy, what are you doing? Going under the house like that, you could get stuck under there. I want you to meet someone. "Charlie, this is Spike. He's a good dog."

The porch was a wrap-around, and now we were out of sight of the dogs stuck together. That's when Sara walked around the house, and Spike knew what he wanted. Sara ran to him, and before I could stop her, she ran around the house with Spike.

"Damn it, Sara, you are embarrassing me. What's gotten into my dog? She's usually so sweet; what the hell has happened to her? Don't answer that."

"There's nothing you can do. Once they get a taste for it, they'll never stop. That's what Cole says, anyway." Bailey said, laughing.

"You're married to Cole Reed; that sounds like something he would say."

"Do you know Cole?"

"I haven't seen him since I was a teenager. I used to visit my aunts; they're the Randal sisters.

"Oh, I love them," Bailey said. "They're so sweet. Are they your great aunts?"

"No, they are my regular aunts. My grandmother was in her fifties when she had my father; he was a surprise baby. They think I should stay with Levi so he can help me walk again..." I never had a chance to finish my sentence because Levi interrupted me.

"I will help you, and I'll have you running up the mountain with Bailey; she runs all over this place."

"I don't run that much anymore. I have two children, and, as you can see, another is on the way. But I do walk a lot, so we can walk together as soon as you're able. I usually push a stroller; if you go with me, we can push two strollers."

"I would love to walk with you. How old are your children?"

"Jackie, she's our first child. She'll be two next month, and Grace turned one last month," Bailey said, smiling. Maybe this one will be a boy, but if not, maybe the next one will be. We are going to fill our house with love and children."

"That's the best thing I've ever heard," I said, and quickly wiped the moisture from my eyes. I was the one who chose my path, so what if I wanted to change my mind and have a house full of babies? I was only thinking like this because that doctor said I might not ever have a child. I won't think of it again.

5
STEEL

It had been four weeks since Charlie moved into my house, though not exactly with me, but rather in my house. As I massaged her legs, attempting to coax her muscles into relaxation, I couldn't help but wonder how much longer I could endure the task. My body seemed to betray me once more, as despite my efforts to keep my arousal in check, my libido had other plans. My member strained against my basketball shorts, thankfully loose enough to conceal the evidence of my unwanted arousal.

Contemplating what Charlie might do if I were to pull her into my arms and kiss her, I entertained fleeting fantasies that remained only in the realm of my imagination. She was my friend, and I refused to jeopardize our relationship.

"Here you go, let me wipe the oil off of you. So you don't slide all over the place," I offered, handing her a towel.

"I can finish, thank you. My legs feel so much better. Thank you for getting me back in shape. I think I can handle everything now," she expressed her gratitude, taking the towel and wiping the oil from her legs. "I think I'll do more walking before I stop for this morning. I feel so good; I couldn't have done this without you."

I observed her sigh of contentment and the proud smile that graced her face as she completed her third round of the room.

"You're doing great. How much pain are you experiencing?" I inquired.

"I hardly feel any pain; I feel like I'll soon be running in these hills. I'm so grateful I came here. Thank you for helping me," she responded.

"You're welcome. I must leave on a mission in a few days, but Ghost will be here to help you, if you need anyone," I informed her.

"Tell me about this mission. Do you always go to other countries?" Charlie asked, her head tilted curiously as she watched me.

"No, this time, I'm going to Southern California to protect a woman hiding from her crazy brother, her words, not ours. Their father left her everything, and he's furious about it. He's made three attempts on her life. She said something has been wrong with him since he was born. She said the police couldn't find him, so we provided security. Rebel is with her now, then I'll take over," I explained.

"Why is she staying in the same town? Have you talked to the police?" Charlie questioned.

"She wants to stay there to bring him out of hiding. We haven't talked to the police, and she wants to do all the talking to the police. She said they think she's overreacting. When I get there, I'll speak to the police," I elaborated.

"And you guys agreed with that?" she probed further.

"That's what we have been arguing about. Rebel claims

he hasn't heard her talking to the police once. But he knows she is talking to someone; she goes into her room, and he can hear her on the phone. But he said she must go into the closet because he can't hear what she says," I shared.

"That does sound suspicious. I wonder why their father didn't leave his son anything. Even a small amount to get by on would make sense. We know he's unstable, she said so herself something was wrong with him. He must have had someone taking care of him before their father's death. It must have been their father who took care of him," Charlie mused.

"Why do you think that?" I inquired.

"Well, if the brother was being looked after by their father and the sister didn't want a significant portion of the inheritance going towards his care, she might see it as a way to eliminate him. If he's spotted around the house, you shoot him, thinking you're protecting the woman. Everything gets sorted, and she keeps it all," Charlie explained.

"You have quite the imagination. Do you really believe such scenarios occur?" I questioned her.

"All the time," Charlie replied.

"Do you enjoy being a homicide detective?" I couldn't help but ask.

"I used to love it, catching the bad guys. But now, the cartel has infiltrated everything in Texas. They'll eliminate anyone they see as a threat, and the feds aren't doing much to stop it. Let me tell you, it's a frightening world out there. I'll be relieved when my cousin gets out," she admitted.

"That's right, he's an FBI special agent. So he's infiltrated the cartel. That's dangerous; why would he take on such a risky mission?" I inquired further.

"The cartel kidnapped his youngest sister. Sabrina when

she was sixteen. She and her friend were walking home from school when they were abducted. We managed to rescue her, but I doubt she'll ever be the same. She witnessed her best friend's murder. My cousin wants Ruben dead; he's the one who brutely assaulted Sabrina. Ruben is also the one who wants me dead," Charlie explained.

"So if your cousin kills Ruben, that will solve both of your problems?" I deduced.

"Yeah, I guess it would, even though Marcus will never be able to live a normal life if they find out who he really is. He's in disguise, and hopefully, they will never discover that he's undercover," Charlie responded.

"I hope he does get a chance to kill Ruben since he's the head of the cartel," I remarked.

"He's head of only one cartel. There are many cartel gangs, not just one, as many people think. There are East and West and Border and Central; all of those are different cartels, and they even fight among themselves. They are killing so many young people with fentanyl, and no one does anything," Charlie lamented.

"Do you think you'll return to your job?" I asked.

"I'm not sure what my future holds. Maybe I'll start inventing more things. I have all kinds of ideas swirling in my head. Do you have the name of the woman's brother?" Charlie redirected the conversation.

"Give me a moment; I'll check my file. I'm sure we have that information," I said, retrieving the file and skimming through it. "His name is Nate Lawler. He's twenty-six, and he was born with a disability, which is a developmental disorder. He lives in a home but visits his sister regularly. His father has spent every day with his son. He has the mental capacity of a child," I confirmed, dialing Rebel's number.

"Hey, I looked into the brother; he resides in a care

facility and has the mental capacity of a child," I relayed the information to Rebel.

"What the fuck is going on?" Rebel exclaimed. "I knew something was wrong; I could feel it."

"We suspect the sister wants us to kill him when he visits her on Saturday. His father has probably set up automatic payment for the rest of his life, and the woman wants the money," I explained.

"Well, fuck, I'll call the police and have someone come out here and fill them in without telling her. So, how did you think to check the brother out?" Rebel inquired.

"Actually, it was Charlie who raised the suspicion. She found the whole situation fishy," I admitted.

"Are you talking about Charlie Primrose Randal? Is she there with you? I thought her aunts were taking care of her," Rebel said.

"We decided they couldn't do that after Miss Molly bumped into her wheelchair and sent her careening downhill and into the swimming hole," I replied.

"Fuck, that must have been terrifying for her," Rebel sympathized.

"Yes, I'm sure it was. I'll leave you to close everything up there."

"How did she know about the brother?"

"I'm still trying to find that out. I'll talk to you when you get back. If you think we need to talk to the brother's care facility, can you do that before returning?"

"Yeah, I'll go there after I talk to the police," Rebel agreed.

I turned to Charlie after ending the call. "How did you have a hunch about her brother?"

"As a homicide detective and a former criminologist, I've seen my fair share of murders and dysfunctional families.

Sometimes, my instincts guide me in the right direction. I've encountered situations where families turn against each other over money. They'll kill their grandmother for money," Charlie explained. "You should contact the facility where the brother is staying and ensure he can't leave with his sister if she shows up."

6

CHARLIE

I saw Levi working out with some of his buddies, so I headed to the kitchen for coffee instead of working out. It was seven in the morning, and I almost fell over when I heard someone clapping.

"You are walking without help, and you get better every day. I'm so proud of you. How do you feel?" Bailey said, standing at the stove cooking. I saw Izzy holding a baby in her arms and another sitting on a blanket, playing with a toy. Then Jaz walked in while her boys ran behind her. Sometimes, I forget how large Steel's family is.

"Mom, we're going to find Uncle," one of the boys said as they ran out of the kitchen. I saw Bailey's daughter Jackie follow them, and I picked her up.

"Where are you going, sweetie?"

"Daddy."

"She wants her daddy," I said with a chuckle.

"Yes, she has her daddy wrapped around her little finger. Your daddy will be here in a few minutes. I'm sure they'll smell the food by now."

Five minutes later, they started entering the kitchen.

There were always people coming and going at Levi's house. At first, I was surprised by all the family members who came and went throughout the day. Last Sunday, this place was full of family members, with most of them starting to cook early in the morning. I knew I would miss everyone who came here, but mostly, I would miss Levi. But it was time I went home; I couldn't stay here forever. I was walking all over the place now. I looked at Bailey's babies. I would miss holding babies in my arms.

"Why do you look so sad?" Levi asked, sitting next to me.

I smiled. "I was thinking how much I'm going to miss everyone."

"What do you mean?"

"It's time for me to go home. I've been here for eight weeks. I can get around independently, so I no longer need to stay here."

"You can't go home; what if Ruben has people watching your house?"

"I no longer have that home. My parents sold it, so I'll go to their house until I can find one."

"Stay here. I have to go overseas tomorrow. Sara is going to be having her puppies any day now. You don't want her having them somewhere else. Here, she has all of these people to take care of them."

"You don't think people will think it's strange that I'm still here and can care for myself."

"No, everyone loves coming here and talking to you," That's when I noticed the others at the table. Everyone had stopped eating and was listening to our conversation.

"Why don't you stay around here? Do you miss Texas so much that you haven't considered moving here?" Jaz asked.

"No, I don't miss Texas."

"I thought you would want to live here with your aunts.

They are getting up there in age. They might need someone to help them. I wouldn't say anything because Miss Molly asked me not to tell you. But I think you should know. Miss Hillary fell yesterday and hurt herself. So, Miss Molly is taking care of her."

"What?" I turned toward Levi. "I'll get my things. You have to take me to my aunt's house. They need me."

∽

I LOOKED at Jaz when she stood and made a phone call. She didn't hear me walk up behind her. "I told her Miss Hillary fell, so you two can take it from here. Good luck."

When she turned around, she bumped into me. "What's going on?" I asked.

"Nothing, Miss Molly told me about Miss Hillary. She said to tell Charlie only if she planned on leaving. So that's what I did."

"Okay, good move," I grinned and went outside to find Sara. I found her and loaded her into the back of my truck. Sam jumped in, so I called Bailey out. "What are you going to do about Sam?"

"Sam, you are not going. Get your butt out of that truck," Bailey demanded. Sam jumped down, but he cried. I laughed as I walked back inside and to Charlie's room, where she was wiping her eyes.

"What's wrong?"

"I'm silly; I was just thinking that I would miss you. Who else can make the best coffee in the world?"

"I'm going to miss you too," I looked at her; she was the beautiful Charlie Primrose Randal, standing tall with her cowboy boots and tight jeans on; she had a white tank top with her gun in its holster. She always carried her weapon. I knew it was because she didn't want to risk something happening with the cartel.

"Hand me that bag," I said as I walked up to where she stood and took the bag from her hand. I wiped a lone tear as it rolled from her eye. Then I bent my head and kissed her; it was only going to be a quick kiss. Then she wrapped her arms around me, and the kiss deepened.

I raised my head, and her eyes gazed into mine before she turned and left the room. I chuckled and followed her. "Sara is in the truck, waiting for you."

"Do you want me to watch Mertle and Spike while you're gone?"

"I'm taking Spike with me, and Jaz took Mertle home with her. You can move back here with me as soon as Miss Hillary is well. I miss carrying you around."

She stopped walking, "What are you talking about? I'm not moving in with you."

"Why not? I like you being here."

"I'm not going to talk about it right now. My Aunt Hillary needs me, and you are going overseas."

I leaned down and kissed her passionately, and her arms went around me again; I didn't care who was watching us. I was claiming her as mine, and now they all knew it. "We should have done this long before now. Think of all the fun we've been missing," I said, giving her another quick kiss.

I heard a chuckle before she got into the truck. Oh yeah, she was all mine, and I would let her know that as soon as we got back from overseas.

7

CHARLIE

Levi had been gone for a month, and I must confess I missed him. Sara and her puppies were driving me to the brink of insanity. I let them outside for a while to gain some respite from them. Walking further into the yard, I saw someone walking up the hill. I looked and couldn't believe who I saw; my cousin Marcus was here. Something had to be wrong.

"What happened?" I said as I rushed toward him. He seemed surprised to see me running.

"You can walk?" he asked.

"Yes, now why are you here?" I said, wanting Marcus to tell me what happened.

"They know you're alive," Marcus replied, hugging me.

"How do they know I'm alive?" I questioned.

"I don't know. Someone was talking to your mother, and she mentioned that you were doing well when they offered their condolences. It seems like a setup. They know you are somewhere in these mountains."

"Fucking crap, I love it here. I don't want to leave. I might even be in love."

"What? Sweetie, you don't have a choice; they'll be tearing this place apart. You have to leave immediately."

"Let me tell my aunts I have to leave," I hurried into the house. "Aunt Molly, I have to go right now. The cartel knows I'm here, and I have to leave before they start showing up."

I grabbed my gun, some bullets, the hidden money, and dashed outside. Marcus was keeping an eye on something down the hill. That's when I spotted Jaz and the boys running. I looked around and saw the black SUV they were attempting to kidnap Jaz and the boys.

With a burst of speed I didn't know I possessed, I leaped over the fence when I saw Marcus scoop up both boys and shield Jaz and the boys with his body as he aimed and shot one of the men. I ran straight toward the SUV, and I knew what I had to do. I had to let them capture me, or they would harm Jaz and her boys, and everyone else on this mountain. I wouldn't let that happen. They were after me, and I wouldn't let anything happen to the people I love.

"No! Stop, Charlie, don't do this!" Marcus shouted.

"Marcus, keep Jaz and her boys safe!" I yelled back as I charged toward the SUV. I felt the bullet as it pierced my shoulder. I had been expecting it, but it still knocked me down. That's when rough hands seized me, and I was struck on the head, and everything went dark.

"It's about time you woke up. I've been waiting for hours. I thought you were dead, until my sister saw your mother in the library, talking about how good her daughter was doing. I must admit I was surprised. It only took 24 hours to locate you; your mother will be in the hospital for a while."

"You fucker," I shouted before kicking him and knocking him from his chair. I knew I would pay for that, but it was worth it until he kicked my wounded shoulder. The bullet must still be in there. The pain almost made me vomit; I didn't cry out; I would never let Ruben see the pain he caused.

"I'm going to let your shoulder fester until it rots off before I kill you. You deserve a long, painful death, and that's exactly what you will get. It's just you and me, I would rape you, but I hate you too much. I can't stand to touch you," and then he spat in my face.

"I need to get to the hospital," I said to divert his attention.

"Have you heard a word I've said? You are going to die a pain-filled death. I'll strip pieces of your flesh two inches at a time. No one will hear you screaming from here; we're in the middle of nowhere. But first, I need to chain you to the wall."

"What? *How will I get away if I'm chained to the walls*? I looked around, and that's when I realized we were in a windowless basement.

"I see fear in your eyes. Good, you understand how serious I am," Ruben said before putting his fist in my face, and then he kicked me until I blacked out. All my healing seemed to have been in vain.

"When I regained consciousness, I found myself chained to the wall and alone. I hoped Marcus could look after the mountain people with Levi and the Delta Force Guardians gone. Would more cartel men arrive now that they knew Ruben had me? I hoped they didn't recognize Marcus; he had his disguise off. Hopefully, they didn't know who he was.

I tried to inspect my wound, but my restricted movement prevented it. How on earth was I going to escape from here? *Damn, I would love a glass of water.* I closed my eyes when the door creaked open.

A woman entered her eyes filled with fear and sympathy. She was more a girl than a woman, she was maybe seventeen. "Hello, don't ask for my help. I'm just giving you some water, and that's all. Ruben will be back soon, so we need to hurry. Don't let him know I brought you water. After that beating, I figured you'd be thirsty. I hated his brother. He used to rape me, and Ruben did nothing to stop him because that was his younger brother. I'm glad he's dead. Ruben went to get a sharper knife; he said he's going to skin you alive."

"I know he told me. Is there any way you can help me? He has me in these chains, and I can't move."

I saw her eyes darting around nervously. "He has the keys. I can't do anything to help you; Ruben would kill me. He's almost finished with me. I saw him with a couple of younger girls. He hasn't killed me yet because I gave him two sons. I hope he lets me live in a house alone with my sons; I don't want to be shared by all the men again."

"I don't blame you; men can be so stupid. Why don't you kill him, and you and your sons can live alone? If no one likes it, kill them too. I'm sure you've heard everything he's done. Carry a gun with you and shoot them, or take your boys and move far away," I wondered if she knew I was just saying stuff to keep her in here I was so scared, I didn't want to be skinned alive.

"Do you think I can do that?"

"Of course, you can. You have woman power. You are stronger than Ruben because you are smarter than he is," I wasn't sure if she believed anything I was saying. I hoped so, she might be my only way out of here."

"He's back; I have to go."

I must have dozed off because a sharp kick jolted me

awake. Then, a foul breath washed over my face as a hand snaked up my blouse. "Keep your fucking hands off me," I shouted at the man.

"Ruben said you were mine, for now. He found himself a young girl to amuse himself with for a few nights before he finishes you off."

"Stay away from me. I don't want you anywhere near me," He grabbed my hair and pulled my head back, I almost gagged when his mouth covered mine. I couldn't fight back because I was chained to the wall. I saw the woman standing behind him, and then he fell on me, and she pulled him off of me.

"I killed him, and I'm going to kill Ruben when he returns," I couldn't believe she had listened to me.

"Can you help me get out of these chains?"

"No, I'm not ready to do that just yet. I want Ruben to be surprised when I kill him just like this one. He's raped me many times. Now he will never rape again. I like this new me. I should have done this a long time ago."

"Listen, I have to take care of my aunt; she fell and hurt herself, and she needs me," I explained.

"I don't have a key," she replied.

"Could you bring me a hammer? I'll break myself out of here. Please help me," she walked out of the room and returned with a hammer.

I was hammering away when I heard a scream, and then Ruben walked into the room. He started laughing when he saw me trying to break the chains. I was so angry I threw the hammer, and it hit him in the head.

I watched as his body fell to the ground across my legs. I reached for him as far as I could, but my chained hands couldn't reach that far. So I worked him up with my legs until I could grab him; my hands went into his pockets until

I felt the keys. I had the chains off and was running out of the house when I almost fell over the woman who gave me the hammer. She was knocked out on the kitchen floor.

I stopped when I heard men talking; they were coming around the side of the house. I turned around and ran back inside and bumped into someone. He grabbed my arms and pushed me out into the yard.

"Look who I found hiding around the building. She already killed Ruben, so let's get the fuck out of here before they think it was us. I'll contact Juan and let him know what's going on."

"Let me go home. I only want to get away from here," I said, pulling my arm away from the man who picked me up and threw me over his shoulder. He tossed me in the vehicle, and we left.

"Stop fighting, or I'll tape your hands and feet."

"Who are you?"

"Don't you worry about who we are," I felt the vehicle pick up speed as we drove away from the house. Fear and relief battled inside me. I was free from Ruben, but my fate was still uncertain in the hands of these strangers. I thought of Levi, and prayed he would find me soon.

8
STEEL

"What the hell do you mean they took her? Who took who?"

"Don't shout at Jaz; she's been a nervous wreck this last week. Now that you are here, I'll leave to find my cousin," Marcus said.

"Where's Charlie?" I asked urgently

"Have you been listening," I swung my fist, but Marcus blocked it. I looked at him, and realization struck me. "Are you Charlie's cousin?"

"Yes, I am. Now excuse me, I have to find Charlie," Marcus replied.

"Start from the beginning," I said through clenched teeth.

He introduced himself. "My name is Marcus Hernandez. Ruben found out Charlie was here. I managed to warn her, but then four cartel members arrived. I took down one; Charlie managed another, but they took her when she saw them chasing Jaz and the boys. She ran towards the van to distract them, and they seized her."

"They shot Charlie first and knocked her out. I heard them laughing as they took off," Jaz said, wiping her eyes.

"I've got some men working on it. I got a call that Ruben is dead. They said that Charlie threw a hammer at him, and it hit him in the head and killed him."

"Who has Charlie now?" I asked anxiously.

"Another cartel. I'll try to locate Charlie before they sell her."

"You're leaving?" Jaz questioned, looking at Marcus. She grabbed his arm.

"I have to leave. I need to find my cousin."

"Wait, how do you know another cartel has her?" I asked.

"I have informants in the area. They reported she had an infection in her shoulder from the bullet wound. The bullet was still inside before Eli removed it."

"Who's Eli?" I asked. None of this sounded good.

"He's an undercover special agent and one of the guys who found Charlie."

"Can't he rescue her?"

"No, you can't blow your cover when you've spent years gaining the cartel's trust. Eli will keep an eye on Charlie, and I'll get her to safety once I catch up with them."

"The mountain will be safe. We'll bring her here," Steel suggested as he walked away.

Marcus followed him, frowning. "What do you mean 'we'? I have to go in alone. They'll get suspicious if they see me with you."

"They won't know anything if we don't tell them," I replied. "We won't answer their questions."

"Do you really think that'll work? They don't trust anyone; they'll shoot us," Marcus shouted.

"I don't have time to stand around arguing. Take me to them, or I'll find them myself," I said, walking away.

"Who the hell are you?" Marcus demanded.

"I'm Steel, and you're fixing to find out why they call me that. Let's go," I added as I walked onto my porch. Ghost decided to join us.

Ghost looked serious, but I didn't want to risk his life. "Are you sure? Marcus thinks we'll get shot before we even start."

"Yes, I'm serious. Grandpa and his new wife are home; quite frankly, all that kissing and touching from those two give me the creeps. They are in their eighties, for Christ's sake."

I chuckled, recalling their last visit. Glancing at Marcus, I asked, "Where do you think she is?"

"Eli didn't have time to tell me anything. I assume they're still in the desert, so that's where we'll go. I can't be seen with either of you, and I have to disguise myself first. We'll take Charlie's plane to save time."

"Charlie has a plane?" I asked, surprised.

"She claims it belongs to her father, but we all know it's hers. Charlie invents things; did she mention that?" Marcus asked.

"She said she'd invented a few things but said her father is the main inventor," I replied, letting Marcus know Charlie had mentioned it.

"Charlie has always let her father have the credit for their inventions, but she's the true inventor. She's probably thinking up something right now," Marcus explained as he applied a liquid to his hair with his fingers, and it turned blonde.

"Did she invent that hair product?" I asked.

"Yeah, but only for me. She said she'd never sell it," Marcus said, quickly transforming his appearance. I watched as he put something on his face, making it look thinner and older.

Four hours later, we were driving down a dusty desert road. I glanced at Ghost, whose hair and beard now had streaks of gray. Ghost smiled at me. "You look quite different with that red hair."

I chuckled, recalling the box of hair dyes Marcus had. Eventually, the jeep slowed, and we turned into a driveway leading to a decrepit house that looked on the verge of collapsing. "Is this where Charlie is?"

"I hope so," Marcus said, getting out of the vehicle, "Let me handle the talking," he said as we followed behind him.

I knew that wouldn't be happening. He knocked three times, and someone opened the door. "Who are they?" the man enquired, blocking the entrance.

"Don't worry about us," I replied, pushing past him—two others were in the hallway with their guns drawn. I ignored them and walked to where the men sat in the living area. The three men leaped to their feet; guns pointed at me.

"Where the hell is Charlie?" I demanded. I heard Marcus growling as one of the men cocked his gun. My fist landed in his face, and he dropped to the ground while the others aimed their guns at my head.

Marcus shouted for everyone to stop, and they backed off. He looked at me with frustration. "I told you not to start a fight. What's your problem?"

"My problem is that Charlie isn't here," I said, turning to the men. "Where is she?"

"She's not here anymore. She was, but she stole our jeep

and left," the man I assumed was Eli, the undercover FBI agent, explained. He seemed ready to explode.

"We came here because we heard she was here. How long ago did she leave? Marcus asked. "Why didn't you go after her?"

"Two guys went after her, but we had no vehicle," Eli replied.

"Come on, let's go," I said, heading back to the vehicle. We returned to the vehicle, and the man who spoke to us got in the back seat.

We drove for ten minutes before Marcus broke the silence. "How did she get away? Didn't you reveal your identity to her?"

"I removed the bullet from her shoulder and gave her antibiotics. She knew who I was. She thought there were too many others here. Her fever was high, and she was sleeping. While we rested, she slipped away. What could I do? Ruben's men have been here with me."

"What took you so long to get back here?" Eli demanded.

"I was watching the people on the mountain in case more cartel members showed up there. I knew you would take care of Charlie. Apparently, I was wrong."

"She'd be dead now if I hadn't removed that bullet from her shoulder. How could I have known she'd sneak off in the middle of the night?"

"It's Charlie Primrose; you know how she is," Marcus replied.

I wondered how Eli knew Charlie so well. Were they friends?

"Who are these guys?" Eli demanded.

"They're Charlie's friends."

9
CHARLIE

I managed to pull the vehicle over onto the side of the road, feeling a searing pain throbbing in my shoulder. The urgency to escape capture consumed me; I couldn't wait to drink something cold. My throat was so dry I couldn't even swallow, and the dust seemed to infiltrate every pore.

I opened the car door and clumsily fell to the ground, driven by a desperate need for shade. Regret filled my mind as I realized I should have stayed inside the vehicle and turned on the air conditioner. Why had I forgotten about the air conditioner? What the hell was happening to me? I should have stayed where Eli was. Why did I leave? He would have kept me safe until Marcus or Steel found me.

Remembering the other men's sinister words and intentions flooded my thoughts—they planned to sell me to another group as Ruben's killer, to the highest bidder. My eyelids grew heavy, and I could no longer keep them open.

∼

"Mama, hurry, here she is. See, I told you I found a dead woman here."

"Fetch your brother. She's still alive, and we must see if we can help her," she said, her concern evident. "Look at her, she's burning up; what is this? It looks like a bullet hole. That's why I am leaving this place as fast as I can. This place is pure evil."

"Jackson, help me get her inside the house. She seems like she's running from something or someone. After we get her inside, I want you to take that vehicle and hide it. I know we were leaving today, but we can't leave her alone."

"Mom, what if she dies? Will someone blame us?"

"No one will blame us because we won't let her die. She'll come with us when we leave."

"Can you hear me?" I repeated my question to the woman for what felt like the hundredth time. Two days had passed, and she still hadn't stirred. Her fever had subsided slightly, giving me hope, but I needed her to wake up. I wanted to get my boys away from this border town, which had become even more menacing with rival cartel gangs vying for dominance.

"Mama, a man is coming."

"You boys get in there with that woman. I'll talk to the man."

I opened the door before he had a chance to knock. "What can I do for you?"

10

STEEL

I was taken aback when the door opened, revealing a determined woman ready for action. "I'm looking for my friend. She's injured and on the run from the cartel. Charlie was kidnapped and brought here. I have to find her and take her back home. Have you seen a woman come this way?"

"Why do you want this woman?"

"I told you, because she's my friend, she has been shot in the shoulder, and she might have a fever. I have to find her."

"Mama, more men are coming."

I glanced at the child and then back at his mother. "Those are my friends. We're here to find Charlie," I said, trying to find out if she knew anything.

"They look like the cartel to me," she said, eyeing Marcus and Eli suspiciously.

"We found the vehicle, so she has to be here," Marcus said; he did look like a cartel member.

"Marcus is an FBI special agent. He and Eli are undercover, and Marcus is Charlie's cousin."

"Follow me; the woman has a fever. I managed to bring it down, but she still hasn't awakened. My son found her by the roadside; he thought she was dead." She led us inside, and I rushed to Charlie's side when I saw her.

"Hey, sweetheart, can you wake up for me? We need to leave this place. I examined her wound, and it appeared infected. Ghost, I need to clean this wound and drain the infection. Can you gather everything I need?"

"The problem with opening it is you'll have to push the poison out," Eli commented, touching the area around her wound. "I find it strange that the antibiotics didn't work," he added, frowning.

"I found these pills in her pocket, but they're not antibiotics; they're sleeping pills."

"These aren't the pills I gave her. Those bastards must have switched them."

"I'll open her wound, and then we'll all leave," I looked at the woman, "You and your boys need to get out of this place."

"We know that, but we couldn't leave her here alone."

Ghost handed me his sharpened knife, its tip still glowing from being heated. My hand trembled as I carefully pierced her skin, causing infection to ooze out. I continued until it stopped. Then I lifted her and carried her outside.

The woman followed. "You and your boys can go with us. Where were you planning to go?"

"I thought somewhere far away from the border."

"We live in the Appalachian Mountains in Kentucky. It's a beautiful place. Have you thought about living in Kentucky?"

"Kentucky sounds like a wonderful place to start anew."

"Are we going home?" Charlie whispered.

"Yes, we are going home. How do you feel?"

"Not so good. I'm glad you're here with me. I knew you

would find me. Ruben is dead. Eli is somewhere around here."

"He's here."

"Is Marcus here?"

"I'm right here."

"Marcus, I killed that bastard for you. It's over," Charlie drifted back to sleep.

I looked at the woman who had saved Charlie's life. "If you make it to Kentucky, look us up. We live in the Appalachian Mountains in a fantastic community. We're almost all family there, and that keeps everyone from talking about the others," I said with a smile, seeing a chuckle escape Charlie's lips.

I worried about the infection, but I held her in my arms and knew she would be alright. I leaned down and kissed her soft, dry lips. The thought of losing her had terrified me; I knew I never wanted Charlie out of my life. I wouldn't let her know it would scare her off.

∾

I WATCHED as Allison checked Charlie, ensuring she was following everything she was supposed to do. "You're completely healed now. So, what's your next move?"

"I was considering moving back in with my aunts, but they love having Jaz and the boys there. I'm so grateful that she was here to help with Aunt Hillary. I think it's a win-win for everyone; there's more space for the boys to play, and my aunts have young ones to keep them feeling youthful."

"You'll be staying at my place. I want to make sure there's no longer any threat from the cartel," I said looking at Charlie.

"Steel, you don't have to worry about me and the cartel,"

I smiled wondering if Charlie had noticed, she'd started calling me by my Delta Force name. I remember it started when the car cut us off, leaving the cartel behind, and I sat her on the seat and walked up to the men in the vehicle, and one fist each in their face and knocked both men out.

"You have all of these puppies to find homes for, and they're all settled in well here, so you should stay here until they're all adopted," I knew if I brought up Sara, she would stay here. I waited for her to answer me.

"Alright, I'll stay here until the puppies have a new home. Thank you for having me; it gives me time to figure out what I want to do with my life. I've never had so much time on my hands."

"I noticed you've been working on something in the garage. I'm glad you are making use of all that space. Who needs a four-car garage? Are you working on an invention?"

"At the moment. It's just something in my head. I hope you don't mind me borrowing your tools."

"Of course not. Feel free to use anything you need. I've got more tools than anyone could ever need."

I was surprised at how many tools you have. Are you secretly a mechanic?" I teased, amused by the look on his face.

"My father handed down those tools, except for a few I used to make birdhouses. If you look at people's porches, you'll find quirky looking birdhouses hanging there I made for everyone, when I was in the tenth grade," I chuckled, remembering how I thought these birdhouses were a work of art as I gave everyone their gifts.

"I'm surprised they still have them on their porches; I painted each one with different colors," Steel said I noticed he was a little embarrassed telling his story.

"Of course, they still have them, they cherish them

because they're homemade gifts. Nothing could be better than a homemade gift. I would cherish any homemade gift made by someone I care for. But then again my father does make me things all the time, sometimes I redo them," She laughed, "don't tell him I said that."

I knew what Charlie would be getting from me for Christmas – a finely crafted birdhouse. I can make a much better one at thirty-six than I did at sixteen. I pulled Charlie close and looked into her eyes. "Charlie, it's been two weeks since we got back; I've waited this long to kiss you, so can I kiss you now?"

She wrapped her arms around my neck. "It's about time."

I laughed as I pulled her closer and kissed her passionately only to be interrupted by a throat clearing.

"Sorry to interrupt you two," Bailey said smiling, "Charlie and I are watching an older movie called Love Story. I've heard it's really good, and it's about to start."

"I glanced at Charlie and chuckled before giving her another kiss. I'll see you in a few hours. I have a meeting with the Delta Force at Rebel's house. Enjoy your movie," I said bestowing one more kiss before leaving.

I watched as Charlie picked up the baby and nuzzled her neck. "Come on, everyone, let's watch a good movie."

You can imagine my surprise when I returned a few hours later, to find Charlie sitting on the couch, tears streaming down her cheeks. "What's wrong? Sweetheart, why are you crying?" She shook her head.

"Sad movies always make me cry, that's all. It was a sad movie."

I looked at her and knew it wasn't the movie that had moved her to tears. "Talk to me."

"Bailey is so lucky; she has those babies; she gets to

cuddle and kiss her babies all day. I'll never have that because the doctor told me I'd never have a baby due to the damage from that accident."

I lifted her onto my lap. "Sweetheart, was he a gynecologist?"

"No."

"Well, there you go. He can't definitively say whether you can have children or not."

"There was another doctor who also said I most likely won't be able to have a child. I never spent much time around babies, so I didn't know what I was missing until I held one in my arms."

I kissed her forehead, took her hand, and led her to the bedroom. "We are going to make love. I'll lock all the doors so no one can disturb us. I've been waiting for this since I pulled you out of that cold water," she chuckled and took my hand.

"I'll walk with you so I don't back out."

11

CHARLIE

To say I was nervous was an understatement. The truth was, I had never made love with a man. I hadn't even tried using a vibrator, despite my friend telling me I should give it a try. That was in college. I almost had sex with the jerk I dated, but I thanked my lucky stars that I hadn't gone through with it.

I stopped by his home to surprise him, and a coworker was with him; they were both too busy to notice I stood in the doorway. Until I made a noise, his excuse was that he had to find sex somewhere else since I wouldn't put out. I didn't acknowledge him, I turned around and left. He hurt me, but not enough that I would talk to him.

However, everything was different with Steel. He was a man I yearned for with every fiber of my being. I wanted him to take me right then and there; I didn't even care if we were in a bedroom or not. By the time we made it to Steel's room, I was ready, and so was he.

He gently pulled my top up over my head, and I didn't feel self-conscious about my scars; Steel knew each and every one of them. He had massaged them, and I thought he kissed them once, although I was almost asleep, so I couldn't be sure if it was real or I imagined it.

How was I going to tell him that I was a virgin? Would it change his desire for me? Should I reveal this now or wait until we were both naked? After all I have seen naked men before. I'm a homicide detective, so I've encountered all kinds of people. "Stop thinking Charlie Primrose Randal," I whispered to myself, "Just tell him."

He picked me up, and I wrapped my legs around his waist as he tenderly took a breast into his mouth. My mind seemed to leave me at that moment; I didn't know what to say or do. I had no intention of disrupting what he was doing; I decided to discuss it with him later.

He slowly undressed me and then himself. My eyes widened when I got a look at his impressive arousal. How on earth was that going to fit inside me? He was huge. Maybe I should say something now instead of later.

Before I could make up my mind, he lifted me up and gently laid me on the bed. Then, he leaned down and whispered, "I'm going to savor every inch of you sweetheart. I've wanted to do this since that first massage." He wanted to taste me, I thought, and I instinctively raised my hips as his lips touched my most intimate spot. He took my legs and placed them over his shoulders. As his tongue began to work it's magic, I didn't know what to do. My body seemed ready to explode when his finger joined in. I cried out for more.

"Let it go, baby. Your body is ready to release. Let it go, sweetheart," I wasn't entirely sure what I was supposed to let go of, but I was ready. And then, my body exploded in a breathtaking climax. So this was what an orgasm felt like? It was mind-blowing; it was beyond anything I had ever imagined; I started to cry like a baby, tears streaming down my face. Steel came up and looked at me, concerned.

"What's wrong?"

"It was the most beautiful feeling I've ever experienced."

"You've never had an orgasm before?"

I felt like a freak. "No, I'm still a virgin."

"What? Why didn't you tell me? I would have been more gentle."

"Don't you dare stop. I want to make love with you."

"Sweetheart, I'm not going to stop; I'm going to stay with you all day, making love to you. You are ready right now because you are wet enough for me to slide inside you."

"You look really big. Do you think it will fit," I asked, my voice trembling.

Steel chuckled, "It will fit perfectly."

He slowly pumps his finger in and out, and I gasped, "You doing good?" he asked.

"Yeah, I'm ready for you," when the tip of his erection touched my sex, I may have panicked for a moment. "How am I doing?" I ask like a kid wanting to know how good I'm doing.

"You are doing fucking fantastic, this might burn a little, but that feeling will go away."

"I'm not sure that big thing will fit inside me."

"It was made for you," he says as he puts his finger back down there, playing with my sex again. I felt like I might orgasm again. Oh my God! I cry out as he pushes inside me. He stops for a moment.

"How am I doing," I asked again.

"You're doing amazing," he replied, and the stirring inside me intensified as he picked up the pace. Our lips met in a passionate kiss, and he moved even faster. My body shuddered as I experienced another orgasm. Steel continued to move, and my mind was in a blissful haze. I wrapped my legs around him, urging him on, and as he reached his own climax, he cried out.

Steel kissed my eyes, nose, and lips before rolling on his side, bringing me with him. We shared a deep, passionate kiss, and he held me in his arms as we both drifted into slumber. I couldn't help but chuckle; I had completely worn him out.

Gently disentangling myself from his embrace, I realized I needed a shower. While I was preparing dinner, Steel entered the kitchen. He immediately pulled me into his arms, dressed casually in low-slung sweatpants that left little to the imagination, clearly desiring me. If it weren't for his parents sitting at the table, I might have abandoned the stove and led him back to bed.

"Hello, son," Steel paused to give me a quick kiss on the nose before turning to acknowledge his parents at the table.

"Hello, Mom and Dad," he greeted them warmly. You both look great, nicely tanned. Jaz mentioned you're moving back to the mountain. It's a good thing you didn't sell your home."

"I heard you've been taking care of Charlie while she's been injured. That was incredibly kind of you," his mother chimed in. "I'm sure Charlie wants to return to her aunt's house."

"No, Charlie's not going anywhere," Steel asserted as he took a seat at the table, wearing that familiar, determined expression I'd come to recognize.. "Charlie, you didn't have to cook dinner."

"I know I didn't have to, I wanted to make spaghetti for everyone."

12

STEEL

I couldn't believe my parents wanted Charlie to go back to her aunt's house. I glanced down at my attire and realized I was underdressed. "I'm going to get dressed. I'll be right back."

"Steel, I invited Jaz for dinner so she could visit her parents too. All of you can spend time together. Marcus will pick me up, and we'll head to the hardware store while you spend time with your family. There are a few things I need," Charlie mentioned.

"I'll take you to the hardware store. I have a few items to pick up as well. Mom and Dad can catch up with Jaz and the boys. I can visit them anytime now that they've moved back. Let me get dressed," I couldn't resist leaning in to kiss Charlie before I left the room. "Don't leave without me."

I couldn't help but smile at the worried expression on her face. After quickly changing, I returned to the kitchen, Jazz and the boys were already seated, along with Marcus, who appeared quite uneasy. Charlie took the garlic bread from the oven. Dinner is ready. "Jaz, if you'd like to take over, I will leave you to it."

I grabbed a piece of bread as we walked out the door. I swear Marcus was sweating when we got outside. He paused and looked at us. "I'm heading out. I have some matters to attend to in Texas. You take care of yourself, Charlie. Is there anything you'd like me to pass on to your parents?"

"I thought you would stay a while. Aunt Hillary was so happy having you stay with them. What about Jaz? Does she know you're leaving?"

"Yes, I've spoken to Jaz; I told her we would keep in touch. I'm an FBI special agent and will always be an FBI special agent. I've been undercover with the cartel for two years. I don't belong here."

"You have to make your own life decisions," Charlie offered, "I believe you are wrong; you belong anywhere you want to live."

"Marcus," as we all turned, Jaz ran out and wrapped her arms around Marcus. "I'm going to miss you, so much."

We watched as he lifted Jaz, and she wrapped her legs around him, sharing a heartfelt, passionate kiss. What the hell have I missed? Marcus walked away with Jaz clinging to him, so they could talk privately. I watched as the two talked; Marcus wiped the tears from her cheeks and kissed her again before putting her down and walking to his truck.

"Are you in love with Marcus," I asked Jaz as she stood there watching Marcus drive away.

"I don't want to talk about Marcus," she replied, walking back into the house. I turned and walked back to Charlie. "I'm sorry I dozed off earlier; I want you in my bed tonight if that's where you want to be."

"Your parents have a key. I was getting out of the shower when your mom walked into the bathroom. I nearly had a heart attack."

"I'll get the key back," I assured her, pulling Charlie into my arms. "What do you need from the hardware store?"

"Nothing, I just wanted to get out of there quickly. What do you think about Jaz and Marcus?"

"Jaz hasn't been involved with anyone since her husband died. I'm pretty sure he never kissed her the way Marcus just did. Maybe he'll come back. How are you feeling?"

"I feel wonderful."

"No regrets."

"Never."

"What would you like to do?"

"I'll spend some time with my aunts for a while. I need to check on them anyway. I haven't spent much time with them. Would you like to come with me?"

"No, I'll go back inside and visit my parents. They're probably bombarding Jaz with a million questions. I should lend her a hand after seeing that sad look on her face." I leaned in and kissed her, our eyes locking. "Do you ever take your gun off?" I asked her.

"Yes, when I go to bed, you won't have to worry tonight. I'll place my gun on the nightstand," Charlie said, kissing me.

"I can't wait for tonight. Are you too sore?"

"Not much; I'm sure it'll all be gone by bedtime. I'm going to walk to my aunt's. I'll see you later."

"I'll pick you up in an hour."

"Alright, that will be perfect."

13

CHARLIE

"Charlie, having Jaz and her boys here has been an absolute delight. They enjoy it when I read stories to them, and we have a great time playing kickball. I must admit, playing with them makes me feel like I've rolled back the clock twenty years," Aunt Hilary enthusiastically shared.

"I feel the same way. I sincerely hope her parents don't persuade her to move back into her small house," Aunt Molly chimed in, her expression on the verge of tears. "It brings back memories of your Dad running around everywhere. He grew up so quickly; I wish he could be little again. I cherished those moments when I cuddled with him during nap times."

"Have you told Jaz that you want her to stay here?" I inquired.

"Yes, we've both told her we would love for her and the boys to remain. I'd hate for those boys to move out," Aunt Hillary confirmed.

A smile spread across my face; it was evident my aunts cherished having the boys around the most. As I glanced around, I noticed toys neatly stacked in the corner of the parlor, and the room had been tidied up of anything breakable.

"Now, please have a seat. I'm eager to hear all about your relationship with Steel. Have you seen his parents?" Aunt Molly asked.

"Yes, I had just finished showering when the door unexpectedly swung open, and there was Steel's mother, just as surprised as I was. I let out a scream, and she quickly retreated. When I entered the kitchen, I found them both there, so I decided to start preparing some spaghetti; it seemed like the natural thing to do, I explained, prompting laughter from my aunts.

"Where was Steel during all this?" Aunt Molly inquired.

"He was still asleep at the time. He later strolled into the kitchen wearing a pair of sweatpants that hung low on his hips, shirtless, with his tattoos proudly on display. He looked incredibly handsome. Without even noticing his parents at the table, he walked over, pulled me into his arms, and planted a kiss on me," I recounted.

My aunts erupted into laughter, "I wish I could've been a fly on the wall to witness the entire episode as it happened. So, what's happening between you and Steel?" Aunt Molly asked, her tone turning serious.

"Auntie, I'm thirty-three, and I'm still trying to figure out where this relationship is headed. It's all quite new to me. I will say that Steel is the only man I've ever been with, which might seem unusual at my age," I admitted.

"Nonsense! There's nothing strange about it. I was forty when I had my first experience with a man, and it wasn't the best, he didn't let me feel any pleasure, but the next one was much better. So I was quite happy when he convinced me to spend a weekend at a hotel," Aunt Hillary shared, wearing a smile that left me stunned.

"I was nineteen when I had my first experience, and I enjoyed it. But I also had strong feelings for the man, so I'm not sure if that makes a difference," Aunt Molly added. My ears were on fire, and I wanted to poke my eyes out after seeing those smiles on my aunts' faces.

I was not going to swap tales about having sex with my two aunts, who were close to eighty. It was my turn to talk because they looked at me like they were waiting. "I won't discuss Steel anymore with you; it makes me feel strange. But I will say one thing. I only felt pleasure," I declared, prompting my aunts to break into applause.

"Let's eat dinner. I made a delicious roast. Jaz said she would only eat a little spaghetti; she loves roast."

"Did you know Marcus was going back to Texas? I was a little surprised to see him picking up Jaz, and they shared the most passionate public kiss I've ever witnessed."

"They are deeply in love," Aunt Molly shared.

"He'll be back. He loves those boys and Jaz, but Marcus feels he's unworthy of someone like Jaz. He spent two years with that ruthless cartel, and it will take some time before he realizes his true worth. He's dedicated to saving women and children from those monsters," Aunt Molly said.

"I hope he comes back. This roast beef smells delicious; I love it with all the trimmings. I cooked them some spaghetti for dinner."

"What made you start cooking dinner in that uncomfortable position? I would have gone out the back door."

"I don't know. I'm sure Steel's parents thought I was a crazy lady rummaging through all the drawers for pots and pans. I couldn't find any meat, so it's meatless spaghetti. At least I managed to make a tasty sauce for them, and garlic bread, I've never been into cooking."

"You are a kind soul for even thinking of making dinner

for them. I always knew you were a good girl. When I see you sitting here like this, I can't picture you as a homicide detective. Except for that gun attached to your hip."

"Thank you, Aunt Molly, but I'm a grown woman now. I'm not sure what I will do anymore; I used to know exactly what I wanted for my life."

"That's right, Molly, she's a woman now," I held my breath, waiting for Hillary to add to that sentence, but she didn't say anything else."

"Tell me about my Dad when he was little?"

"Molly spoiled him rotten; he would cry over the smallest things, and she'd come running."

"I didn't like anyone picking on my son," I looked at her, my mouth fell open, and Hillary stared down at her plate while Molly remained tight-lipped.

"Aunt Molly, are you my grandma?"

"Oh dear," she said, wiping a tear from her cheek. I jumped up and hugged her.

"Tell me what happened."

She shook her head and covered her face with her hands. "I was so scared; I had three months left in my final year of college when I couldn't hide it any longer. I tried to pretend everything was the same. Joesph visited me every week and would show up out of the blue. I should have realized he was using me, but I was convinced he loved me more than his wife. That's what he always told me."

"When I told my parents about the baby, they were ashamed and embarrassed, and they came up with the idea of me going away to have the baby. I was twenty-one when my baby was born. I wanted to go away and live with him alone somewhere. But before I could do that, my mother told the entire mountain she had a surprise baby. Without knowing she was pregnant."

"My only chance of being with Benjamin was to live at home. I still worked at the Bank since that was my plan. But I could never claim my baby. I had to swear on the Bible never to tell anyone. Hillary refused to move out, because she was so angry over how my parents went behind my back and claimed Ben as their son. You are the only person who knows."

"What about Joseph? Didn't he know?" I asked.

"Yes, but he refused to acknowledge the baby was his. He had his own family with two kids, so I never saw him again. Except when he walked into the bank that day. We didn't talk, and I refused to look at him again," Molly said.

"That is so unfair. I've had a grandma all this time. My father never knew you were his mother," I wiped the tears from my face. "My Dad thought his grandparents were his parents all these years. This whole thing is the saddest thing I've ever heard. It isn't fair to any of you," I said, wiping my eyes.

"Tell me, who raised my Dad?" I said, hugging both of them.

"Hillary and I did everything with him. I loved him so much. I used to beg Hillary to go out there and find a husband, but she didn't want me to be alone. I have the best sister in the world. I hated my parents for what they did. I should have moved away with him anyway. They found a way to keep me here, and I was stupid."

"When Ben got older, he would tell me that I didn't have to play with him all the time if I didn't want to," Molly cried into her hands. "The only thing I wanted to do was be with him. It feels so good telling you about this. My God, I hated this secret. I wanted to tell your dad he was my son, but I didn't want him to feel shame. That's what my parents said he would feel."

"My grandma, Aunt Hillary, and I had cried so much that we were completely exhausted when Jaz and the boys returned. Steel was also there; I hugged my grandma, looked at her, and smiled. I will see you tomorrow, Grandma. I guess you know I'm calling you grandma from now on."

"Finally, it's out in the open," Jaz said, smiling.

"What, how did you know?" Grandma asked.

"I just guessed because you loved Benjamin so much, I knew how it felt to love your child," My heart went out to Jaz as my grandma cried some more. My tears started to fall. I looked at Steel, "You're going to have to wring me out; I've cried since I got here; I have a grandma," I said, crying. I saw his eyes well up; he pulled me in his arms and hugged me. I hugged my grandma and Aunt Hillary goodbye. I looked at Hillary. "So, you are my great Aunt?"

"Yes," she said as she began crying, "you don't know how good it feels letting this secret out. It has eaten me alive since Ben was a little boy with no father who would play ball with him."

Steel put his arm around me. "Come on, sweetheart, let's go home."

14

STEEL

"I believe Miss Molly should be the one to inform your father that she's his mother. It should come directly from her."

"I understand, you're right. It's challenging to keep this secret now that I know the truth. It's scorching today; let's head to the swimming hole," Charlie suggested.

"Alright, let me change into my swimming trunks."

"I'll put mine on under these shorts. This is going to be a lot of fun."

"Leave your gun behind; I'll keep you safe."

"I know you will. It's just a habit that will be hard to break. I've had to look over my shoulder for so long. Today I'll leave it at home. Hopefully, I won't need it," I noticed the concern on her face. I bent my head and kissed her gently, "I will always protect you, sweetheart."

"I know," Charlie replied before putting her arms around me. Charlie and I haven't exchanged 'I love you,' I want to be completely sure that our love is strong enough to sustain us for the rest of our lives.

We walked to the swimming hole, finding it deserted. I

jumped in the water and was surprised it was still so cold. I laughed when Charlie leaped in and shouted because it was freezing. I swam over to her and held her close. "I'll keep you warm," I whispered as my hand slid inside her bikini bottom.

"You certainly know how to warm me up. That feels amazing," Charlie said as my finger found its way inside. I took her bottoms off and tossed them on the water's edge. This swimming hole was on my property, and I felt safe making love to my beloved here. I had already removed my trunks and tossed them on a nearby bush. When Charlie wrapped her legs around me, I entered her. She threw her head back and moaned loudly. I quickly realized Charlie made passionate noises during lovemaking, which only intensified my desire.

I moved us closer to the waterfall for more privacy just in case someone happened upon us. Our lips locked as she reached her climax. Then, it was my turn to cry out with my release, and our lips remained locked as I held her close. I gazed at her, and she giggled.

"What's so amusing?"

"Our clothes are on the bank, and a dog is inspecting your trunks. Hurry and retrieve mine before he runs with them," Charlie said, pushing me toward the opposite shore. No more than Charlie said that, the dog barked, snatched my trunks, and dashed away.

"Hey, bring my clothes back," I attempted to exit the water faster, but Charlie's laughter made me laugh too. "If you don't stop laughing, I won't retrieve your bottoms," I teased, pulling her closer.

"Are you looking for these, cousin?" Bo Taggert appeared, holding up my shorts as his dog stood beside him.

"I knew I shouldn't have given you that dog. What are you doing away from home?"

"I'm looking for little Will; he never leaves the property, and now we can't find him."

"Throw me those shorts, and I'll help you search," I caught them as he tossed them over. My heart sank when he mentioned that his Will was missing. Charlie swam up beside me.

"How long has he been missing?" She asked Bo.

"It's been almost an hour now; I better get going. Call if you spot him."

"I will; I'm going to call in more people," I yelled as Bo walked away.

"Thank you. We need all the help we can get," Bo said over his shoulder.

"Where do you think he could be?" Charlie said.

"I don't know, but I hope he has fallen asleep somewhere close by."

"Maybe he has; let's get dressed so we can join the search. It terrifies me when kids go missing."

"Yeah, me too." Thirty minutes later, we had twenty more people helping us search, and more hours passed. As I hiked up the mountain, I encountered two of my brothers running toward me. "Did they find him?"

"No, someone took Caleb when he and Cruise were playing together."

"What? How could this happen? If someone took Caleb, then someone must have taken Will. I grabbed my phone, called Bo, and quickly headed to find Jaz. I needed all the information she had. "Have any of you seen Charlie?"

"Yeah, she was with Jaz, but I don't think she's still there. She went to grab her gun and hunt the man down. She believes he might have Will too."

"Why the hell wouldn't she wait for me?"

"She said she would have waited for you, but she felt time was running out for those boys. You should have seen her. She had her gun, another one tucked in her belt, and two knives in her boots."

"Call your wives and instruct them to lock their doors and keep the children indoors. We don't want any other kids to go missing. It's crucial that we spread the word about this man who's taking our children. This is crazy. Do you know which way Charlie went?"

"No, what's your plan?"

"I'm going to talk to Jaz, and then I'm going to kill that bastard that has taken two of my family members."

"Allison mentioned that someone might be staying at the old Johnson cabin. She saw smoke coming from it. She also said it's barely standing, ready to collapse with a strong wind. Do you think the kids could be there?"

"I'll head up there. Did you tell Charlie someone might be up that way?"

"She was there when Allison told us."

"Fuck," I spotted Jaz standing in the middle of the road, in tears. "Jaz, we'll find him. I'm sure Will is with him too. I promise we'll find him. I need to ask Cruise what the man looked like."

"Cruise said the man was old, like Grandpa, and had a hairy face. That's all he knew."

"Okay, go be with him while we search for Caleb and Will," I took off, walking uphill, when she called after me.

"Levi, find our babies; they're scared, just like their mothers."

I nodded; I was afraid my voice would tremble too much trying to talk. People were scattered all over the mountain; I couldn't fathom why we hadn't seen any sign of the boys. As the sun began to set, I spotted Bo walking down the mountain.

"What do you think? How did this man manage to elude us so quickly? He couldn't be on foot."

"You're right; he couldn't have gotten away that fast if he were on foot. Cruise mentioned he ran with Caleb, while Caleb screamed. He had to have a vehicle; that's the only way he could have gotten away. He may not be from this area. Did you check the Johnson shack?"

"Yeah, there were a couple of runaway teenagers in there. I sent their ass home and called their parents. I'm so scared," Bo wiped his eyes with his sleeve. I can't believe my baby has been taken, I can't go home until I have Will in my arms," Bo said.

"Stay with me, and we'll find them together."

"Where's Charlie?"

I was wondering the same thing. I'm sure we'll see her soon. We continued knocking on doors three hours later, ensuring the boys weren't inside someone's home. Most of the people in the homes cried when they answered the door. At two in the morning, we ran into Marcus, which surprised me. I didn't know he was here.

"My team is here, with me. I'm going to kill that bastard when we find them. If he takes little boys now, he'll always take them forever. He has to die."

"How did you know about this?"

"I'm keeping a close eye on Jaz and the boys. The moment she called the police, I knew about Caleb. My team and I have been here for hours."

"Have you seen Charlie?"

"Not yet. Look, I have a hunch. Do you two want to see if my hunch is right?"

"Yeah, we'll go with your hunch."

"We'll take the vehicle, and I wouldn't be surprised if Charlie is hanging around there too. We drove only half a mile when Marcus turned off his lights, going another half mile in the dark.

I was surprised when we arrived at the church. "Why are we here?" I whispered.

Because the priest hired an ex-convict who is a pedophile. He used to work at another church, and instead of going to jail like he should have, they sent him to this church. This came up on our radar. Let's go," We ran up the steps to the church doors, and to our surprise, they were open.

I looked at Bo. "Keep your ears and eyes open. Something is happening here; I can feel it." We had barely walked ten feet when a hand reached out and touched me. I knew it was Charlie before I saw her. I signaled for Marcus and Bo to stop and follow me. We went into another room, and there was Will sleeping on the floor.

Bo dropped to his knees and wept as he lifted his child in his arms. "Where is Caleb?"

Charlie pulled Marcus and me to a corner and explained what had happened. "The priest and the man are in the back with Caleb. I was just going to get him. Let's go get him now."

We moved through the darkness, following Charlie. We could hear someone whispering, and I realized it was Caleb. He was talking to the man. "When my Uncle Steel finds me, he'll kill you."

"Caleb, come away from that man, don't talk to him," the priest said.

I stepped around the door and wanted to shoot the bastard, but not in front of Caleb. "Hello, Caleb. Untie him right now. Charlie, please take Caleb and the priest where Bo is with Will," I knew she wanted to argue, "Please."

"Come on, sweetheart, we'll call your mommy. We will give you ten minutes," Charlie said, looking at Marcus and me.

"Now, Levi, let's let the courts deal with this. I don't want you taking matters into your own hands," the priest said;

"You don't get to talk, Father; you knew about this man and didn't warn the community."

15

CHARLIE

I wasn't surprised to see Marcus there; I'm sure he knows everything that goes on in these mountains. Ten minutes later, Jaz arrived, ready to confront the Janitor. She held Caleb close as tears streamed down her face.

"That man was mean; he hit me. I was playing with Cruise, and that man made him cry because he wouldn't let me go."

"Don't worry, sweetheart, no one will ever take you away again. That man will be locked up in prison," Jaz reassured Caleb.

The police showed up, and I confronted them. "Is it on record that this Janitor is a pedophile? He should have been under constant surveillance. Do the people who come to this church know about this pervert?"

"I didn't know about him, Jaz, is Caleb alright?"

"I told that man you would take him to jail, Uncle Jacob," Caleb chimed in.

Jacob picked up Caleb and hugged him tightly. Yes, this was his nephew; I forget how many Petersons are on this mountain. Steel walked into the room and looked at Jacob.

"We need to have everyone on this mountain investigated. If child molesters live on our mountain, then we all need to know, so we can watch our children closer."

"I agree. Where is he?" Jacob asked.

"The FBI took him," I replied, looking at my brother.

"What FBI?" Jacob questioned.

"Marcus and his team took the bastard."

"Marcus Hernandez?"

"Yes, FBI Special Agent Marcus Hernandez. This turned into a missing child investigation, and the FBI joined in, and had every right to arrest the man. What's more concerning is that the Priest knew this man was a child molester and he didn't inform anyone on the mountain."

I watched Jacob shake his head. "Jaz, did you call Marcus?"

"No, I didn't call him. But he found out about Caleb and didn't hesitate to bring his team to find my baby. Because Marcus loves us, and when he gets everything straightened out, he will return to us. Now, we are going home. Can you let everyone know that Will and Caleb have been found?"

"Uncle Jacob, Marcus will kill that mean man because he loves me," Caleb added.

"I know he does," Jacob said, turning to look at his brother, "Steel, did he at least say where he was taking the man?"

"No, it's out of our hands now. Jaz, can we ride back with you? Our ride has left."

"Yes, of course you can. We'll take Bo and Will home first. I called to tell Grandma and Aunt Hillary, and she has tea and cookies waiting for us. It seems strange calling Molly grandma. In a nice kind of way."

Jacob shook his head. "Do any of you care that I have to lie when I write up my report? And could be fired."

"No," we all said at the same time. "Okay, I'll see all of you on Sunday at Steel's house."

"Why will he see all of you at your house?"

"Because it's the big Peterson family grill. Do you remember I told you how everyone comes to my house for Peterson annual family reunion? That's this Sunday. I forgot all about it. So I guess I'll go to Costco tomorrow. Would you like to go with me?" Steel said casually, like it was just another dinner.

"Sure, I need a few things from there, also. I am completely worn out; I bet I walked thirty miles today. It's hard to believe this day started as a swim at the swimming hole. Thank God we found Caleb and Will," I said, my voice trembling.

Steel drove Jaz's vehicle as she sat in the backseat with Caleb, who was talking a mile a minute about his entire experience today. Jacob took Bo and Will home since he lived near them.

As we pulled into my Grandma's driveway, they were all outside waiting for us. Cruise ran up to his brother; they hugged each other, crying the entire time. I could hear them whispering to each other as Steel picked them up and carried them inside while a tearful Aunt Hillary and Grandma followed behind them.

"Our small community will meet tomorrow morning regarding the secret the priest kept from our town. He knew about this man but was told he was starting a new life. We know that was a lie. He didn't even register with the police like he was supposed to. We can't allow this to ever happen again," Grandma explained. "Now, we will have our tea and cookies."

"Steel and I are going to head on to his house; I'll see you tomorrow," I said, hugging them goodbye. My mind was racing. This is why I was a detective, and I wasn't going to stop; I like catching the bad guys.

Steel's phone rang as we walked back to his place. I couldn't help but overhear his conversation.

"That was Ghost, he said we have to leave in the morning; I'll call everyone and reschedule Sunday dinner for next month. We're going to South Sudan; a family went there on a mission with their church and is now missing."

"How many are in the family?" I asked.

"Five, the father of the wife hired us. He said her husband is always volunteering for these dangerous missions. But when he chose South Sudan, no one could believe it. He made their three children go even though they didn't want to. He thinks the husband has his daughter brainwashed."

"Wow, he sounds like he wants something bad to happen to his family. If I were you, I'd investigate him before you leave. Something doesn't add up. Check if he has an insurance policy."

"Good idea," he chuckled. "Do you always distrust people?"

"I guess I'm guilty of that, I've seen so many bad things happen to people by those who claimed to love them. I can look him up for you; I have Marcus's computer access."

"How is it you have Marcus's computer access?" Steel asked, looking at me.

"When Ruben was after me, Marcus gave me his access so I could stay informed about Ruben and his men if they were in my area."

"Okay, let's investigate him," Steel said, draping his arm around me.

One hour later, I printed everything I could find about George Phillips. "What do you think?"

"This guy is suspicious, I swear, unless you investigate someone you're about to marry, you would never know how crazy they are. I wonder why he didn't spend more time in prison?"

"Something must have happened, to get his case thrown out. Some shady lawyers can make things happen for the right price. That might explain why he relocated across the country where no one knew him. I hope you can find them. You have to be extremely cautious over there."

"I'll be careful. Let's go to bed. What are you going to do while I'm gone?"

"I'm going to Texas. I have to wrap up a few things."

"Please stay away from the cartel."

"I won't be anywhere near the cartel. Don't worry about me. I can take care of myself—most of the time. I'm going to talk to my father about Molly. I'll be back before your return."

"Okay, I won't worry. I thought you had decided to let Molly tell your father," he said, undressing me before we got to the bedroom.

"I'm not going to discuss my grandma and father while you undress me," I said, chuckling.

16

STEEL

The scorching heat was unbearable; I estimated it to be around one hundred and twenty degrees outside and a sweltering one hundred and thirty inside. "I turned to my team and questioned, "Remind me again why we're stuck in this cramped room?"

Ghost glanced at me, his shoulders shrugging in uncertainty. "I have no idea."

"Rebel, why are we still holed up in here?" I asked, growing impatient.

Rebel's voice tensed as he whispered, "Listen, someone's approaching." We pressed ourselves against the wall, weapons at the ready.

Spartan suddenly appeared, staring at us inquisitively. "Why are you all in this room?"

"What are you doing here?" I retorted.

"I received an urgent message that I was needed," he replied, puzzled by our surprised looks. "I rushed here, only to be told that you three haven't left this room since your arrival."

My frustration was building. I demanded, "What the

heck is going on? Let's get out of here. Spartan, you don't have to stay."

"I think I'll stay; something feels off," Spartan replied, his concern evident.

I looked at each man before deciding what to do. "Let's pause and regroup. Our previous plan is out the window. We're going in as Marine Corps Force Reconnaissance Soldiers. We are the toughest of all other soldiers, never forget it. We will make sure whoever is trying to trap us will regret it." I looked at the others, and they held their fists out in agreement. "Does anyone have any ideas?" I heard some snickers from the guys. "Let's get the heck out of this room."

"Let's use the back exit; I suspect the front door is being watched," I suggested as we exited the room. Outside we heard shouting, and a vehicle stood there like it was waiting for us. Without hesitation, we climbed inside, and Spartan hot-wired it, and we got the heck away from there.

"Someone clearly wants us dead, or at least someone wants Spartan dead," I mused. "Is there even a family missing? This entire mission is confusing. I told you, Charlie, and I investigated the husband, who had killed his first wife, but they released him from prison after three years due to a court mishap."

We were all thrown completely off balance by this mission's sudden twist. "But we don't know him, so he's not the one after us. What about Carl Graham, the man who hired us?" I asked, turning to Ghost. "What do you think about him?" I asked, since he was the one who spoke to him.

"He seemed genuinely concerned about his family, even tearing up when talking about his grandkids. I didn't sense any deception," Ghost replied, furrowing his brow.

"Do any of us have enemies?" I pondered. "It's just speculation, but what if someone discovered we were coming here and decided to set a trap for us?"

"I can't think of any enemies I have," Rebel stated. "I might have made a few boyfriends angry because I flirted with their girl, but it was nothing this big. What about you, Spartan?"

"I might have a few but I don't know if they hate me enough to go to such lengths," Spartan replied, scanning our faces. "Let's find the missing family first, and if we encounter someone who wants us dead, we'll handle it like we always do."

"Do we even know where the heck we are headed?" I asked, feeling like we were spinning aimlessly. We'd been here for four days, following someone else's orders. "From now on, we'll determine our direction. We know Carl's granddaughter mentioned heading east, so let's go east and see what we find."

An hour later, we remained disoriented and lost, at least no one was following us. We drove until we ran out of gas, then alternated between running and walking. As the sun rose, casting a beautiful array of colors across the sky, our surroundings grew greener, but the mosquitoes swarmed us, forcing us to cover every inch of exposed skin due to the risk of diseases.

"We have to find a place to rest and fill our water bottles. Hopefully, we'll find clean water," Rebel said, finishing his last sip of water.

Rebel, whose real name was Dash Bellmont, was Spartan's brother, and Spartan's real name was Liam Bellmont. Ghost is their cousin; his name is James Bellmont. We had known each other since childhood, growing up on the mountain, we even joined the Marines together.

"Look, there's a house up ahead with a couple of cows;

they must have water. Maybe we can buy some food from them," I suggested cautiously. We treaded carefully, unsure of who we might encounter, given the ongoing conflict between the Buran and Sudanian armies, making trust a scarce commodity. "Let me do the talking."

As we approached the house, we could hear a crying child reached our ears. I signaled for the others to slow down while I cautiously moved along the side of the house. There, on the ground, sat a toddler, perhaps not even two years old.

"Hello, is anyone here?" I called out. The baby looked at me, stood up, and walked over. She gazed at me as if I were her savior, and her striking green eyes took me by surprise.

Gently, I picked up the child, and Spartan took the lead as we headed for the hut. I felt uneasy about what we might find inside, but I followed Spartan while Rebel and Ghost kept an eye on the outside of the hut.

Inside a young woman lay on a cot. At first, I thought she was dead until her eyes fluttered open. She was scared initially, but her expression softened when she noticed the child in my arms. Then she looked at me and managed a sad smile before speaking in perfect English.

"Her name is Savannah, I named her after her father's homeland. He had planned to take us there, but he was killed. I am dying. God has sent you here to take my daughter home with you. Raise her, and let her know that her mother loved her very much. I held on until I knew she'd be safe," she said, closing her eyes, taking a shallow breath, and passing away as if she had been waiting for us. We tried to revive her, but it was futile.

"Mommy," the child whispered.

I looked at her, feeling uncertain about what to do. She had red hair and light brown skin. "I bet you're hungry."

"I hungry."

"You'll have to take her home with us," Spartan said. It's clear the woman was ostracized from her people because of her child's mixed heritage. That's why she was living out here alone. Savannah would have perished if we hadn't come this way."

I retrieved some jerky from my backpack and offered it to her. She took it cautiously, as if unsure whether to trust me, and began to chew on it.

"I hope she doesn't choke on that," Spartan remarked as we left the hut. "I wonder what caused the woman's death," he added, surveying the area.

"What are you looking for?"

"A shovel; we need to bury her before it gets any hotter."

Rebel and Ghost approached us. "We found the water. What's going on?"

"The baby's mother passed away," Spartan explained, "but before she did, she gave the baby to Steel. As you can see, her father was white. Her name is Savannah after her father's homeland, where they planned to live before he died. So Savannah will be with us."

"Do you have any experience with caring for a child," Ghost asked. "We'll help you."

We buried Savannah's mother. I bathed Savannah, changed her clothes, and we prepared dinner. Savannah climbed on my lap and fell asleep. I took my blanket from my pack and covered her so the mosquitoes wouldn't bite her more than they already had.

Leaning against the hut, and dozed off until Savannah began searching for her mommy. I picked her up and hummed a soothing lullaby until she drifted back to sleep. "What the heck am I going to do with a baby girl?" I whispered to Ghost, who sat beside me.

"Steel, you know more about babies than Viper, and he's got almost three of them. With all of your nieces and nephews that you've taken care of, not to mention those hundreds of Peterson kids that live on the mountain. It's like you were destined to be here in this place."

"It reminds me of that movie I watched with Carrie," I replied, "the one about the dragonfly. The deceased wife was trying to communicate to her husband that she had their baby. He thought the baby had died with her, but the dragonfly wouldn't stop until he went to where she died. The baby was with a tribe in the rainforest or somewhere."

"Geez, Ghost, do you and Carrie watch movies when she visits?" Rebel asked.

"No, Gabe hogs the TV, so whatever he's watching. Most of the time, we just talk."

"Does she still bug you about Allison?" Rebel asked, smirking.

"Rebel, get some sleep; I refuse to discuss Allison with anyone."

"I thought cousins always shared stories," Rebel said.

"Sleep," Ghost growled.

17

CHARLIE

I turned to Marcus once again, seeking advice for the tenth time, "What do you think I should do?"

"I don't even know what I'm going to do, so how can I advise you? Follow your heart," Marcus replied.

"But he hasn't expressed his love for me. I can't just move in with him when I'm unsure if that's what he wants. Sure, he let me stay there, but was it just until I healed? Does he want me there all the time?" I sighed as I sat next to Marcus in my parent's scorching Texas backyard, thinking about my dilemma.

"Trust your heart. That's what I plan to do. Are you in love with Steel? If the answer is yes, then move your belongings into his house, even if he hasn't returned yet. You were living there when he left. So what's all the worrying about?"

"Will you be living on the mountain with Jaz and the boys?" I inquired.

"I don't know what I'll do yet; this is something that I have to spend time thinking about," Marcus replied.

"What happened to the guy who kidnapped the boys? I continued to probe."

"Why are you asking so many questions? Are you trying to chase me away?" Marcus asked with a hint of annoyance.

"No, I was just curious since you haven't mentioned anything about him; after all, he left with you," I explained.

"I don't discuss my work. Now, stop with the million questions. I'm selling my home," Marcus responded.

"Where are you going to live when your house sells?" I pressed further; how was I supposed to find anything out if I didn't ask questions.

"More questions. I haven't decided yet. I'm still weighing my options," he replied.

"Can you believe my Dad already knew grandma was his mother? He said his grandfather told him on his deathbed because he couldn't take that lie to the grave with him. He told my Dad he had nothing to do with his wife inventing that story about being his mother, and he regretted going along with it," I shared, still amazed that my Dad had known all these years and never mentioned it.

Marcus shook his head in disbelief, "Wow, that's unbelievable. People seem to be the same in every generation; you think a grandmother would never do something like that, but sure enough, she did. If I get bitten by another bug, I'm going inside."

"Yeah, let's go inside; I want to see if my Dad is going to visit my Grandma. I think he should. What do you think?" I asked, wanting to know how he felt about it.

"I think it's up to him, so don't try to pressure him into going," Marcus advised, glancing sideways at me.

"Marcus, why would you think I would pressure my father? For Pete's sake, I would never do that," I declared, unsure if I would or not.

I heard him chuckle and ignored it. "We are a mess, aren't we? Here we are intelligent and good-looking, yet we are sulking because we wish we were on the mountain with that happy Peterson family. For me, the issue is the idea of a large family. Steel wants lots of kids, and I can't give him that. My body will never experience a child growing inside me."

"You never know miracles happen all the time," Marcus said, wrapping his arm around me.

I stopped walking and stared into Marcus's eyes, surprised to hear him talking about miracles. This was the same guy who wouldn't hesitate to kill a child molester or drug cartel.

"I haven't always been this way. Remember when we used to discuss our dreams? You wanted to paint beautiful landscapes, and all I wanted was to join a band and sing. The problem was I couldn't carry a tune, and you didn't know how to paint," Marcus started to chuckle, which soon turned into hearty laughter, and we both found ourselves unable to control it.

I could barely speak, still chuckling. "How do you even remember that? I was ten, and you were fourteen; I remember I broke my arm when I tried to use those homemade wings I made and tried to fly off the roof."

"I never told you, those wings actually worked for a few seconds before they slammed into the ground," Marcus admitted, I couldn't believe you did that. You were so brave."

"Because I believed they would work. That was crazy; I used to invent things way back then until my mom threatened to give me away if I didn't stop creating stuff. So, I took a break for a few years anyway."

"I always thought you were amazing, and I even tried to train my mind into invent things. But all I got out of that was a headache. Everything in my life changed when I was sixteen, and Mateo was shot and killed while he was walking down the street, minding his own business," Marcus said somberly.

"Mateo was such a great person; he loved his little brother Marcus. I remember he wouldn't let your father swat you if he was around," I reminisced.

"I never told you this, but after you tried to fly off the roof, he told me to never try any of your inventions if I knew they were dangerous," Marcus revealed.

I chuckled, realizing that this was the first time Marcus had ever mentioned Mateo to me. "Yeah, he was amazing. Mateo had more patience than anyone I knew."

"He was the best, and I still miss him," Marcus said, I pretended not to notice Marcus wiping his eyes, as I too wiped away my tears.

"Is that why you became an FBI Special Agent?" I asked.

"I was quite inexperienced when I joined the FBI. I thought I could catch all the bad guys, but for every hundred good guys, there are a thousand bad ones. It's a never-ending battle, and many good people lose their lives trying to apprehend the bad guy."

"Yeah, that's why I became a homicide detective. But now we're adults, we've become wiser. I still have a desire to invent things, but I need some assistance. Would you consider being my partner?" I asked.

"What about your dad? I thought he was your partner?" Marcus inquired.

"No, my dad isn't my partner; he's helped me when I was a child, now I'm grown."

"Can I take some time to think about it?" Marcus requested.

"Of course, I'll give you six months to decide. In the meantime, I can start jotting down my ideas. Let's go see what's for dinner. The aroma is tantalizing," I suggested, heading toward the kitchen.

"Did you ever learn to cook?" Marcus asked.

"No, why bother learning to cook when I can simply order my food already cooked?" I replied.

"Do they have delivery on the mountain?" Marcus wondered.

"I never considered that; I usually eat someone else's cooking. So if I decide to return to the mountain, I'll continue with that. Steel is an excellent cook. I thought he would be back by now; it's been four weeks since he left. I hope he's safe. That place is dangerous' I've been researching it online."

"Maybe he's at home waiting for you," Marcus suggested.

"He would call me if that's what he wanted. I won't dwell on it tonight; let's grab some food."

At five in the morning, I had made up my mind—I was going to Sudan.

"You can't go to Sudan!" Marcus protested for the hundredth time.

"Why not?" I challenged.

"Because it's dangerous, and you are a woman. I have to put my foot down and firmly tell you, 'Hell no, you are not going to Sudan.'"

18

STEEL

Ghost came to a halt, turning toward the group, his hands on his hips and an unmistakable anger in his gaze. "We've been here for four weeks, and three people claim to have seen these kids, but no one saw anyone with them. Where would the parents be? It says the kids are twelve, fourteen, and sixteen; it's unusual for them to be alone without the parents. Where in the world are they?"

"I agree; this is strange," I chimed in. "Let's go to the next village. If we don't hear something there, we'll consider leaving. Savannah deserves to be in a loving home where she can play instead of on my back all day. I'm sure if there are white people around here, someone would know where they are. We're not getting any leads. We keep hitting dead ends."

Spartan, always the one who spent the majority of his time thinking, looked at us. "If we have not found them in another week, we should seriously consider leaving. I'm still trying to unravel who sent me an urgent message to come here. I haven't seen anyone who has attempted to kill me. So what is the purpose of my presence?"

"Who knows," Rebel muttered. "I've never been on a mission where we didn't have leads to a certain place where we could find more information out. We also need another vehicle."

"I'm in agreement," Ghost added. "This time, we'll see if we can buy one instead of borrowing it."

"Two hours later, we approached a small village. It was small, but there were kids outside, rather than playing they were working. This pattern seemed consistent across all the villages we had passed through."

"As we got closer and observed them, a sense of unease settled in. They all appeared sickly. I covered Savannah's head with a blanket, and we all shielded our faces, careful not to touch anything.

Approaching the first person I saw about the white kids. I stood six feet away. She pointed to a hut on the edge of the village, and we made our way there. Calling out, I asked, "Hello, are there any Americans in there?"

A boy about sixteen stuck his head out, "Yes, who wants to know?"

"Your grandfather hired us to bring you home. We've been searching for you for weeks," I replied, the other two stepped out of the hut. "Are any of you sick?"

"No, we've avoided the village because we could see that people here were sick. We need to leave; these people have been dying," the oldest boy explained.

"What are your names?" I asked.

"I'm Michael, this is my sister Melanie, and our brother Kevin," Michael said, putting his backpack on.

"We won't take any chance with sickness. Let's keep a safe distance of six feet. Where are your parents?"

"We haven't seen them in six weeks. They left us in the middle of the night. They got on the bus and drove away without a care in the world, leaving their children behind in a hostile country."

I exchanged glances with my team, unsure what to say. It seemed the kids were fortunate that their father hadn't harmed them, as he had done to his first wife. The thought of their mother's survival seemed unlikely.

"We have a long journey ahead. Are you three up for it?" I asked.

"We've been walking for weeks, so let's go," Michael replied. I noticed the youngest, Kevin, looked a bit flushed.

"How are you feeling, Kevin?"

"Okay, my throat is a little sore, but I'm okay."

Damn, just as I suspected, they were sick. We'd need to find a vehicle; they wouldn't be able to walk for long without collapsing, especially the girl who didn't seem to be doing well.

"Is that a baby under that blanket?" Melanie asked.

"Yes, her name is Savannah, and she is my daughter," I explained. I might as well get used to telling people who Savannah was, since I would be raising her.

"You brought your baby daughter over here with you?" Kevin questioned.

"No, I found her here, and her mother gave her to me before she died."

"Why is her head covered up?" Kevin inquired.

"I don't want her to get sick; she's just a baby, and it's hard for her to fight off illness."

"Da," we all smiled. Savannah started calling me Da when I told her who I was.

"Yes, sweetheart, Da is here."

"Boo," the team and I chuckled because we knew she wanted to play peek-a-boo. "You guys keep moving ahead. I'm going to check on Savannah." I reached behind me and gently lifted Savannah over my head. Her tiny legs got stuck, and Ghost rushed back to help, freeing her legs from the holes I made in my backpack for her. He couldn't help but laugh when Savannah playfully grabbed his face.

"Gos," She said.

"Yes, it's Ghost," he chuckled as he handed her to me, and she responded with giggles and a tight hug.

"Hungry," she said. I offered her some water and pulled out another piece of jerky. Savannah started making bubbles with her tongue, a clear sign that she was tired of jerky. Ghost, ever resourceful, retrieved a granola bar from his backpack, catching her attention.

"Where did you find that?" I inquired.

"It was in the bottom of my bag; I crumbled it up so she could eat a small bite," Ghost explained.

"Watch out, or I might start thinking you're going soft, like us Petersons," I teased, observing Ghost feed Savannah a bite of the sweet granola. She had it in her mouth and then looked up at Ghost. Before we knew it, she snatched the bag from Ghost's fingers.

I watched Ghost pry it out of her baby fingers; there was a tug of war for a moment or two before Ghost got it back. He glanced at me with a twinkle of amusement in his eyes. "I'll never be as soft as a Peterson. Here, take this; you can feed her, she might bite my fingers off."

"Hey, sweetie, if you like this granola, let me give you a bite, but don't grab the bag," I said, eventually deciding to feed her the entire bar because she was hungry. Once we got her home, she'd never go hungry again.

I felt as if I already loved this child, like she was meant to be mine. When we get home, I'll have some papers drawn up saying I was her father. One thing about being as high up in the Military as we were, I knew people who could make me a birth certificate that no one questioned.

As we found a spot to rest for the night, I gave Kevin and Melanie an antibiotic, hoping it would help them feel better. Michael sat alone, gazing into the distance. After Savannah had fallen asleep, I sat down next to him.

"How are you holding up?" I asked.

"I think our parents left us here intentionally. My father started acting strange when I was seven. I told my Mom, but she ignored me, and he began volunteering for these mission trips, even though he wasn't religious."

"How did he manage to persuade churches to take your family on these trips?" I inquired.

"I have no idea."

"I suspect he wanted to leave us to each place he took us, but my mother still had a voice and refused. It's been five years since we've been on a mission trip, and I had a bad feeling about this trip. That's why I called my grandfather."

"Have you ever heard them talking about something like this?" I asked.

"Recently, I heard them whispering, but I couldn't make out what they were saying. My brother and sister feel the same way. I wonder where our parents are?"

"We investigated your father; he killed his first wife. But he only spent three years in prison because of a court error."

"What? Oh my God, we need to hurry and warn my grandpa. He might go after him, so he will get his money."

"We've already informed your grandfather about everything; I heard a loud noise and saw headlights in the distance. "Come with me," I said.

"Spartan, we're about to have company," I alerted the team. I placed the kids near an abandoned hut and completely covered a sleeping Savannah. I couldn't risk anyone seeing her; I wouldn't take a chance on something happening to my baby girl.

As the vehicle approached, we spread out. They pointed guns at us, apparently considering taking us as captives. This was not a good situation. Just as they began shouting for us to raise our hands, I heard her before I saw her—a gun aimed at Savannah as she walked toward us.

"Da," I ran and shielded her, taking the bullet in my back. I tucked Savannah under me. Spartan shot the attacker and another man before Ghost and Rebel killed the other men. Ghost bent down to assess the damage.

"Where are you hit?" he asked.

"My back. We need to get in that vehicle and get the hell out of here. You'll have to carry me; I can't move my legs."

"Da," I kissed the top of Savannah's head, and her tiny hand reached out to pat my face.

"Let's get out of here," Ghost shouted, and the kids ran to us. "We'll lay you in the back seat." Spartan reached down and carried me to the vehicle. There were three seats; the kids crawled in the back, and I was in the second row with Ghost and Savannah.

We drove half the night when Spartan pulled over. "We need to take a look at your wound."

"Let's wait until we reach a village; there's nothing can be done now. Listen, you guys. If something happens to me I want you to give Savannah to Charlie to raise. You can take care of her birth certificate."

"We'll handle everything until you're out of the hospital," Ghost assured me before sleep overcame me.

I woke up when the sun was high overhead. It must be around noon; my lower back was killing me. I saw Ghost glancing at me. "What time is it?"

"Two-thirty. There's a town up ahead where we can get

some gas and food. It would be good if we could find a room so I can get that bullet out. How are you feeling?"

"My back is killing me, but at least I can feel my legs. That scared me there for a moment or two," I said, looking around for Savannah and spotting her on Rebel's lap, her eyes fixed on me. I smiled, and she responded with a sweet smile of her own.

"We're approaching the town now, the largest I've seen since we arrived. I wonder if they have a hospital," Spartan remarked.

"Let's find a room where Ghosts can attend to my back. I don't want anyone who doesn't know what they are doing touching me."

19

CHARLIE

"Wow, this is truly an eye-opener, seeing how these poor people have to live. I believe coming here was a mistake."

"That's exactly what I warned you about. But would you listen to me? No, you didn't. So I had to accompany you. I couldn't let you make this journey alone. Honestly, my bed feels like it was crafted a century ago; it's as if it's made of straw."

"I know; I was planning to see if we could switch rooms; mine doesn't have a door. I mean, who doesn't have a door at the only motel or whatever this is," I responded, looking around the area. "Where should we begin our search for Steel? Let's see if we can find a place to grab a meal."

As I turned a corner, I accidentally bumped into someone. My instincts kicked in as I stepped back, meeting Spartan's surprised gaze. He held a baby girl who gave me a warm smile.

"What are you doing here?" Spartan asked with concern. "I was worried when I didn't hear from Steel. Where is he? Is he injured?"

"Yes, we just arrived in this town. We've been pursuing those kids and just now arrived here like an hour ago. Steel was shot in the back by some rebels who aimed their guns at this little one. Steel shielded the baby from the bullet."

"Take me to him. How severe is his injury?"

"Ghost is going to remove the bullet. I've been searching for some antiseptic."

"Let me grab my bag. I brought various emergency supplies. Tell me about the baby. Her eyes are stunning."

"This is Savannah; her mother passed away moments after we found her. She managed to share the baby's name and that Savannah's father was planning to take them to his hometown of Savannah, Georgia. Unfortunately, her daddy also passed away, just like her mommy. Before her death, she entrusted the baby to Steel to raise."

"Poor little sweetheart, come on, let's hurry; Marcus can assist Ghost, he went to medical school. How serious is the injury?"

"When he was first injured, he couldn't feel his legs; that's not the issue now. The problem now is that Steel is trying to reach you before the surgery, and he couldn't contact you. So now he can talk to you in person, and we can get this finished."

"Well, let's hear what he has to say."

"Here we are," we entered a dimly lit room, not suitable for surgery. I looked at the man lying on the bed. When he saw me, he seemed startled, then angry.

"Please don't give me that look. You didn't call, and I felt you needed me," I walked over and kissed him. "Let's move him outside for the surgery. Then we'll leave this place. "What did you want to tell me?"

I wasn't certain if he would respond, but he did. "I

wanted to tell you that I love you, and if anything happens to me, would you raise Savannah for me?"

"Firstly, I love you too. I don't want to hear any more about dying, but of course, I would raise Savannah. Let's get him out of here. Spartan, you can give Savannah to me to take care of while you help carry Steel into the daylight, so you can see better."

Savannah gazed into my eyes as I held her. "Savannah, what a beautiful name. Let me look at you. You're perfect."

"Why are you crying?" Steel inquired as they were carrying him out the door.

"I'm crying because I love her," I replied, tears streaming down my face. Savannah's tiny hand reached up and patted my cheek.

"You're going to scare her," Marcus said, frowning at me. I glanced over at him, and his eyes were teary.

I blinked away my tears and fetched my bag. "Grab that table, and we'll put that mattress on it, Ghost; you should find whatever you need in my bag," I said. Savannah turned her head so she could see my face. I looked at Steel; he was observing us. I moved closer to him and bent to kiss him; this time, it was longer than before. "I love you, Steel; you will be fine. I won't accept anything else."

"I love you too, sweetheart."

"Da."

"Yes, da loves you too. I'll talk to you later today."

"Alright, I'm going to bathe Savannah and find her some clothes. Does she have any clothes?"

"No, I've washed what she has on a few times, but that's it," I watched as his eyes slowly closed. I took Savannah, and we went to find something for her to bathe in. I eventually encountered someone who fetched me an old metal tub. I had it placed in Steel's room since my room lacked a door, and then he started bringing water.

When I first attempted to put Savannah in the tub, she seemed frightened of the water; I wondered if she had ever had a bath. I added some of my pleasantly scented soap, and once she mustered the courage to sit down, she loved it. We were both soaked, and I had never had so much fun. She didn't even complain when I washed her hair.

I dressed her in one of my t-shirts, and she looked adorable. But what could I do about her underwear? While I was contemplating, Savannah walked outside and peed next to a tree. I quickly picked her up, then realized she must not know what a toilet was. I would teach her things she needed to learn; after all, she was just a baby.

I fashioned some makeshift underwear for her from another t-shirt, sewing them with the thread and needle I always have in my bag. One skill my mother made sure I could do was sewing, which has come in handy with one of my inventions.

After combing her hair, I emptied the tub of water outside. Then we sat down, and she fell asleep in my arms. I knew tears streamed down my face, but I couldn't stop them even if I tried. I now had a baby, one that I loved immensely. This was why I felt the need to be here; it was not only for Steel but also for Savannah.

I must have fallen asleep. When I opened my eyes, Marcus stood in the doorway. "How is he?"

"He's sleeping. We're leaving while he's still sleeping. I came to tell you to gather your belongings. Are you ready?"

"Yes, we'll take the bus I spotted parked up front. I'll go get it right now," I said, getting up.

"Rebel already secured it. We're packing our things as we speak."

"Alright, I'm ready. Did you manage to remove the bullet?"

"Yes, everything looks great; I'm sure he'll be sore, which is why we're leaving now so he can sleep through the transfer to the plane," Marcus replied.

"Are you coming with us to the mountain?"

"No, I'm not ready for the mountain just yet. That is such a big decision; I want to make sure I make the right decision for Jaz and those boys," Marcus explained as we walked to where the bus was. I knew Marcus wanted to be on the mountain, but that was a decision he would have to make.

"I'm sure you'll make the right decision," I said.

CHAPTER 20
STEEL

I SUDDENLY FELT a sharp pain in my back as I attempted to stretch, and my memory of what had transpired came rushing back. I found myself lying on a small bed within an airplane cabin. Glancing around, I could see the guys and the kids sound asleep, but I couldn't spot Savannah and Charlie. Marcus turned his gaze towards me.

"How are you feeling?" Marcus inquired.

"I'm doing alright, just a little sore. I feel like my muscles are protesting, almost like I have the flu," I replied. Then, Charlie approached me and gave me a kiss.

Charlie's expression made it clear that she had something important to say, and I braced myself for it. "You need to go to the hospital," she said firmly. "I'll take Savannah to your house and look after her until you're back. There must be a reason you're in so much pain, so you have to see a doctor."

"I agree," she looked surprised that I agreed with her. "Thank you for taking care of Savannah. Is someone picking us up?"

"Yes, Viper and your father will be waiting for us. Your dad will take you to the hospital, and Viper will take us to your house."

"Charlie, thank you for everything. I love you."

"I love you too. You don't have to thank me for anything." I reached out and pulled her in for a kiss.

Upon our arrival at the airport, there was an ambulance waiting for me. I would have preferred to ride in my father's vehicle, but it seemed I had no say in the matter. Hopefully, I'd be able to go home after seeing a doctor.

Ghost and Rebel spoke with the kids' grandfather, explaining everything that had happened. Ghost later reported that the grandfather was so angry he feared he might have a heart attack.

"Dad, let me introduce you to the newest member of our family. This is Savannah Peterson, and she's your new granddaughter."

"She's beautiful. Hello, Savannah, I'm Grandpa."

"Papa."

"Yes, Papa."

"I'll explain everything to you after we get to the hospital. Charlie is taking Savannah home, so she won't have to stay at the hospital."

"How are you feeling?"

"I feel fine, except my muscles ache, and my back is sore where they removed the bullet."

"That sounds normal, and I'm sure everything will work out. I'll follow the ambulance and see you at the hospital."

Two hours later, I could feel steam practically coming out of my ears. "I am not staying here," I told the doctor, standing with his hands on his hips. I had gone to school with Jeff, and one of my cousins had married him. Several of my cousins were also present, working as nurses.

"Are you here to learn about your condition or to tell me you know more than I do?" Jeff replied. "Call Charlie and tell her you'll need to stay the night, or maybe a few nights. You still have poison in your body. We need to treat you before you can leave."

"Damn it," I sighed, looking at my cousins. "Why are you three just standing there staring at me?"

"We're concerned about you because the family reunion is next Sunday, and we always have it at your home. You need to get better unless you think Charlie can handle it on her own. We've already put it off for six weeks."

They were pushing me into a corner, and the only right thing to do was to cooperate. "Alright, Jeff, you win. I'll stay here until the infection is gone."

"No, you win because you're the one with the poison in your body," Jeff said with a smirk.

Before getting hooked up to anything, I insisted on taking a shower. I felt filthy, and my hair needed a good wash. "I'll catch up with you girls later at the reunion," I told my cousins, hinting for them to leave.

"Um, Steel, I'm your nurse," I looked at Shelly as if she were crazy. "Do you want some assistance with your shower?"

"Out," I said, pointing toward the door. All three of them giggled like schoolgirls as they left my room. I slowly made my way to the bathroom in my room and turned on the shower. I stripped and stepped under the soothing spray of water, closing my eyes and perhaps letting out a relieved sigh.

I shampooed my hair three times, finally getting rid of

the unpleasant odor clinging to my body. I wished I could linger in the shower forever, but my cousin interrupted, urging me to get out so she could begin administering the antibiotic drip.

"If you don't come out, I'm coming in," she threatened.

"Alright, I'll be right there."

"There's a clean gown on your bed; I'll be back in five minutes. Your dad went home and said he'll talk to you tomorrow."

Once I was back in bed, Shelly walked in, with a smile. "I had them send up some food. I figured you'd be hungry. I ran and got some of my sweet tea from the nurses breakroom.

"Thanks, this looks great," I said, taking a long sip and smiling. "This tea is delicious. You always were the best sweet tea maker in the family. How's everyone doing?"

"Thank you, everyone is fine. I visited the Randal sisters' home yesterday for lunch. They adore Jaz's boys. Hillary told me that ever since Jaz and the twins moved in with them, they've been able to visit so many people. She said they haven't been this happy since Ben lived at home. The news is spreading on the mountain that Miss Molly is Ben's mother."

"Yeah, I heard about that."

Shelly changed the topic. "So tell me about your latest mission."

"Do I ever tell you about my missions? No, I don't. That reminds me. Can I use your phone?" She handed her phone to me, and I called Reaper, another Bellmont cousin to Ghost.

"Hey, Reaper, we need someone to watch the grandfather at all times, until they find the parents."

"They found the mother; she was dead."

"That doesn't surprise me. Is anyone with the kids and their grandfather?"

"Yes, I'm with them, right now."

"Good."

"Are you still in the hospital?" Reaper asked.

"Yeah, until this infection goes away. I'll talk to you later," I said, hanging up and returning Shelly's phone to her. "Damn, I don't like being idle."

The following day, I woke up to the bright sun streaming in, surprised that I had slept so long. Glancing at the wall, I saw that it was already eleven in the morning. It was probably the first time I had ever slept this late. I stretched and realized I felt much better. Today, I would finally be going home to Charlie and Savannah. As I looked around, I saw them both standing in the doorway, smiling.

I almost didn't recognize Savannah, dressed in her cute pink outfit with ribbons in her hair. Charlie held a pair of tiny shoes in her hand. I sat up and smiled. "You two are beautiful."

"Savannah doesn't like shoes. She prefers to go barefoot," Charlie explained. I pulled Charlie closer and kissed her. "Savannah, do you like these pretty shoes?"

"Mine."

"Yes, they are yours but don't you want to wear them? Let me put them on you."

"No, hurt me," Savannah protested. I kissed her little feet and chuckled. "It might take a while for her to get used to wearing shoes."

Charlie asked, "How are you feeling."

"I feel great, I'm sure I will be able to go home today. I'll call Jeff and find out when he'll be here. How's everything at home?"

"Everything's fine. I managed to find homes for Sara's puppies, and your family were all at your house cleaning."

"What time did they show up?"

"Around four-thirty. Bailey did warn me that they would be there today; she just didn't mention the exact time. I heard the vacuum running, which scared Savannah, but no one was more surprised than Sara and Mertle, who were sleeping in our room. When Savannah cried out, the dogs started barking."

"That sounds like it might have gotten noisy."

"It was, but we all survived. Savannah made lots of friends, and everyone loved her. Plus, your house is spotless. Next Sunday is going to be a great day for the Petersons."

20

STEEL

THE BARBECUE WAS TEEMING WITH PETERSONS, AND EVERYONE had a great time. We had the family football game, laughing between our skinned knees and elbows. Charlie wore a look of surprise as people kept showing up throughout the day. Savannah became the center of attention; she was passed around for everyone to meet. Not one of my relatives asked how she came to be my daughter.

I watched as Charlie laughed at my Aunt Hailey's dirty jokes. And she did nothing when my Uncle Pete, who had too many beers, kissed her cheek. She fit in with everyone, and I was going to ask her to marry me. I loved her, and I didn't want to lose her. Like a person in a daze, I walked to where she stood with all my family around her.

She turned her head, met my gaze, and asked, "Why are you looking at me like that?"

"Charlie Primrose Randle, will you marry me?" I asked. "I love you more than anything in this world, and I want to spend the rest of my life with you by my side, growing old with you. What do you say?"

"I say yes, I will marry you," Charlie replied, covering

her face as tears welled up, while every family member there applauded. I pulled both Charlie and Savannah into my arms.

"We will get married today; Viper can officiate," I announced. "Someone find Viper."

Charlie looked at me like I was crazy before she smiled, adding. "Yes, this is the perfect time to marry. Let me change into a dress, and you find Viper," she said, kissing me and then Savannah's cheek, as she put her into my arms. "Savannah, Da and Mommy are getting married on your birthday. Isn't that wonderful?"

After she left to get ready, Ghost approached me, and he looked too serious for a barbecue and a wedding. "What's up?"

"I was wondering if you've looked through those papers I gave you?"

"What papers? Can we talk about this tomorrow? I'm getting married in thirty minutes."

"Sure, but we do need to talk."

"Alright, we'll talk tomorrow. Come over after lunch. Dude, I'm getting married!"

"I know this is fantastic. I'm so happy for you and Charlie; today is the perfect day for a wedding with everyone already here. I'm genuinely happy for you. Here comes Viper."

Viper chuckled as he slapped me on the back. "So, you're going to bite the bullet and get married?"

"I wouldn't call it biting the bullet. I call it the luckiest day of my life. You were the one who swore never to get married," he laughed because he knew I was right. "Let's get this wedding started before my bride changes her mind."

Ten minutes later, Charlie approached me with

Savannah in her arms, and a momentary foreboding washed over me, and I shook it off.

I glanced at Ghost; I turned to see what he was looking at it was Allison, I wondered if he still loved Allison Reed, Viper's sister; we all knew those two had been in love forever. I don't know what happened between them; it was none of my business.

Savannah came into my arms, and we stood together as a family while Viper officiated the ceremony, amid cheers and applause from our relatives.

We stood together as a family as Viper pronounced us husband and wife, and everyone started clapping and whistling. I looked at My wife, and she had tears in her eyes. Charlie smiled and wiped a tear from my cheek.

"I love you, sweetheart, and I will show you how much I love you every day for the rest of our lives."

"I love you too; I promise I will try my hardest to be a good wife," I chuckled, as did anyone in hearing distance. I put my arm around her, and we turned toward our family as they congratulated us.

It was late when everyone left; Savannah was sleeping in the room next to ours, Charlie was in the shower, and I joined her. I pulled her into my arms as she wrapped her arms around me. We made love in the shower before I carried her to bed, where I showed her how much I loved her.

Her scent surrounded me, and my hands ran down her body. Charlie is the woman I love more than life itself. She's my wife for the rest of my life.

Blood pounded in my ears as loud as the rain that slashed against the windows. Charlie rose up on tiptoe to meet me more than halfway as I bent my head and touched my lips to her warm lips. I devoured her mouth and found out we were both hungry for each other. My tongue plunged between her lips.

Unreserved fire and passion met me head-on. My hands ran through her hair, and I crushed my mouth to hers. Our naked, wet bodies melted against each other. Hunger surged inside us. When we landed on the bed, I was careful not to crush my body onto Charlie, I held myself above her.

"No, I want to feel your body touching mine," she whispered. The touch of her hands so warm on my skin sent sensations straight to my center and made me ache as a slight sound escaped her lips.

I kissed her neck and looked into her eyes. "We are going to take our time, sweetheart, so lay back, and let's enjoy each other."

I slid my hand over one curved hip. Over the smooth skin, her hips lifted when I pulled her against my hardness, pressing it into her hip.

Charlie ran her hands across my chest, and my muscles quivered at her touch. My hand slipped between her thighs, and she cried out on a half sob of pleasure as I touched delicate, aching flesh.

I have never felt this way with any other woman. We made love throughout the night. When Charlie woke up, I lay on my side, watching her sleep. She smiled. "Was I snoring?"

"No," I replied, smiling. "You're beautiful. Want to shower with me?"

"I was hoping you would ask me that question."

Charlie stretched and held her hand out for me to pull her out of bed. I pulled her into my arms and kissed her. As I led us to the shower, our bare bodies wrapped around each other.

I didn't know her body could be so sensitive. Just a little

touch from me and her body would orgasm. She cried happy tears and tears of fulfillment. I kissed her everywhere when she cried tears of satisfaction. I tried to calm her tears. My heart expanded in my chest with love for Charlie. I whispered my love to her as we made love. Then we heard a little voice calling for mommy. Charlie chuckled as she got out of bed.

"Here I am," Charlie said, slipping my shirt over her head. She was gone a few minutes, and then she carried Savannah back into our room; she had a huge smile on her face. We loved cuddling with the baby in the mornings. She was such a magical joy to both of us.

My phone rang as I got out of bed; Charlie had taken the baby into the kitchen to feed her. "Hello."

"I didn't want to call you, but I had to leave for San Francisco. I wanted to remind you to go through those papers."

"What papers are you talking about?"

"I grabbed a bunch of papers and other things from the hut where we found Savannah. I think they might have something to do with her Dad, who is buried next to Savannah's mother. I got everything I could find and put some in your backpack. I also put some in Spartan and Rebel's backpacks. There was a shoebox full of them, and Spartan said he took the papers from his backpack and put them on his dresser."

"Okay, I'll go through them today. Why are you in San Francisco?"

"Spartan had this strange call saying if he loved her, he should come to San Francisco to save her. We have no idea what they were talking about, but we're here. The call made Steel anxious for some reason, so here we are."

"That sounds like another weird call for Spartan."

"That's what we thought. We'll keep our eyes peeled in case someone shows up. We'll see you in a few days."

"Okay, I'll see you then. We need to find out who is pulling Spartan's chain."

"I agree."

21

CHARLIE

I laughed as I cuddled with Savannah; I still pinched myself after a month of having Savannah as my daughter. It scared me that someone would come and take her away. I often thought of her birth father's family, wondering if they knew anything about her and what kind of people they were.

I kept having this urge to see who they were. We have those papers that Ghost took from the hut. They have his address where he lived in Georgia. I've been debating if I should investigate them. After all, they are Savannah's grandparents. The only thing that stopped me was they might try to take my baby away from me. Of course, they didn't have to know I checked them out.

While Savannah slept, I sat down at my computer. Steel was called away for a few days, or I would have talked to him about this. I could call him. But what if he wanted to tell them about Savannah?

I sat at the computer and looked at the names on the paper. Gray and Sherry Johnson. I entered Marcus's FBI info and typed in their name, town, and State, and there they were. I was so surprised that they were young. I read everything that was written about them. They married in high school and had their first son, Gregory. They went to college and had six kids over fifteen years.

So they still have children at home. They must have been heartbroken when their son died. I didn't realize tears ran down my face until Jaz came in.

"Why are you crying? What has happened?" I wiped my eyes. "Read this," I said while tears ran down my face.

"I thought you weren't going to do anything about it. Turn it off; if you go see them, they will want to keep Savannah because she is all that is left of their son. You know the courts will agree with them."

"But can I keep Savannah from her grandparents, uncles, and aunt," I cried. Look how young they are. They lost their oldest son, whom they had in high school. I don't know what to do."

"Don't do anything until Steel gets home; talk it over with him. Savannah is also his child. This woman has six kids and will have other grandkids," Jaz said, imploring me not to do anything rash."

"I won't do anything until Steel is home, and then we will discuss it. I don't know why I've been so emotional lately. It's these papers. I feel like I knew Gregory; he was twenty years old when he died. A college kid who fell in love with another college student and he had good intentions to move back to Georgia; they just never got their chance."

"I can't tell you what to do; it's a decision I wouldn't want to make. I know how much you and Steel love Savannah. The grandparents must not even know about her."

"I know. Let's get some ice tea. Where are the boys?"

"My parents took them out for pizza. Have you heard from Marcus?"

"I haven't spoken to him since we went to Sudan together. He had a lot of things to take care of, but I do know one thing: Marcus loves you and those boys. You'll hear from him soon."

"I know he does, and I do wish he would call me."

"He may not be able to call sometimes when he's undercover, and he can't call anyone. We've gone a long time without hearing from Marcus. I don't think he'll be in the agency much longer. He wants to be with you and the boys. You'll see one day he'll surprise all of us and just show up."

"I hope so. I miss him so much. So when is Steel coming home?"

"He said he was going to be gone a couple of days, so he'll probably be here tomorrow," I said when Jaz got up to go home. She returned to her small house, even though Grandma and Aunt Hillary wanted them to stay. She said she didn't feel right living in someone else's house.

It was two days before Steel returned, and he was injured, it wasn't bad, but it could have been. Someone hit him with a bat, which had nothing to do with their mission. They stopped at a bar on the side of the road because it said best hamburgers than anywhere. Someone inside mistook him for someone else and hit him with a bat. Steel turned and hit the guy with his fist, and the man fell to the ground, knocked out. Steel had a misplaced shoulder.

Savannah was so happy to see him; she was talking so fast we couldn't understand a word she said, and both of us laughed. Steel must have seen the tears I didn't let fall because he wrapped his arm around me and whispered, "It'll all work out."

After Savannah went to sleep that night, I told Steel about the Johnson family. How young they were when

Gregory was born, I didn't leave anything out. I cried the entire time because I knew what we had to do.

"We have to take her to see them and see what they say. I can't just leave her there. So maybe they can come here for a while and get to know her. Say something," I said, burying my face in his chest.

"I'm having a hard time right now. Give me a few minutes. Did you print the papers out? Maybe it'll be easier to put it all together by reading the papers myself. Right now, I can't see her with anyone except us. Savannah is my baby. Her mother gave her to me," I got the papers and handed them all to Steel to read. There were pictures I printed out.

I walked outside and let Steel take his time, going through everything. He came out and found me.

"We'll go see them, and we won't call because I don't want to see anything that isn't the real them. Tomorrow is Saturday, and we'll leave in the morning. Is your plane still at the airport?"

"Yes. Let's see if Ghost can go with us. He's good at dealing with people. We will be too emotional to deal with anything," I said, wiping his tears away.

"Okay, I'll call him tonight. Let's go to bed, sweetheart."

I raised my hand, and he pulled me into his arms. "I missed you so much," I climbed into bed and went to sleep. I felt Steel pulling me close to him, but I was so tired I went to sleep.

22

STEEL

I could hear the sounds of people playing out back, their laughter carrying through the air. I was unsure if I wanted not to like them or if I didn't want to like them. These were Savannah's family, and it came to me that I wanted to love them. Ghost stepped in front of us; he was as upset as we were.

A teenage boy answered the door and looked at us. "Is your parent's home?" Ghost asked.

"Sure, I'll get them for you. Dad, some people are here to talk to you," he called out. I had to smile; he did what most teenagers would do, yell for their dad to come to the door. Glancing at Charlie, I sensed her close to tears.

With Savannah in one arm and the other around Charlie, I whispered reassurance. "It'll be okay."

"Hello, how can I help you?"

Ghost stuck his hand out and introduced us to Savannah's grandpa. "My name is James Belmont. This is Levi and Charlie Peterson, and this is Savannah, their daughter. We need to talk to you about your son Gregory."

I observed the man's hand clutch his heart as he uttered,

"Gregory," his voice trembling. It was evident he had no idea about his son. "Do you know where Gregory is?"

I glanced at the man as tears pooled in his eyes. This was worse than I thought. We were about to tell this family Gregory, their firstborn, was dead.

"Why don't we all go inside," Charlie suggested, gently guiding him as we moved toward a sitting room. The house was big and looked like the perfect home to raise children.

"Please tell me what you know about Gregory. We have been looking for him for almost four years. We argued the last time we talked, and he left angry."

"Let's all sit down? Is your wife home?" Ghost asked.

Another woman, bearing Savannah's eyes, appeared, her anxiety noticeable. "What's happening?" she asked, on the edge of fleeing at any moment.

"Sherry, these people have news about Gregory. Please sit with me," the man implored, his wife reluctantly took a seat beside him.

"I don't want to hear what they have to say about Gregory," She looked at Savannah, and her eyes welled up with tears.

"I feared the worst; he mentioned meeting a Sudanese girl and falling in love. Gregory spoke of marriage and plans for the future. He told us he wanted to get married and finish college after they married like we did. Please, tell me everything," Sherry's voice quivered with emotion.

I could see her trembling. Ghost started talking, and then I took over. "We found Savannah alone and crying; she was hungry, filthy, and all alone out there with nothing but a rag covering her. I picked her up and called out for anyone else.

I walked inside this little homemade hut. It was off to itself. I knew the young woman had been banished from her people. She was lucky she wasn't stoned to death. It must have been because she was married, and pregnant that they let her live. There on a little cot, lay this young woman. She looked at me, with death in her eyes, and I knew she only had a moment to live."

She smiled and said, "I waited for you to come for Savannah before I died. I knew you would come. I saw you in the stars. Will you take her home and raise her? She was named after her daddy's homeland. He was going to take us there to live, and then she died, just like that. We buried her next to her husband; I'm so sorry, her husband was Gregory."

Both Sherry and her husband broke into tears. Charlie took Savannah to the window to watch the boys playing basketball, sensing they needed a moment alone. I thought we should leave the family alone for a while, and Ghost and I stood up.

"We'll be at the hotel. Call me when you're ready to talk," Ghost offered, handing her his phone number.

"Da," I heard Savannah's voice, her gaze fixed on the playing children outside. "Play."

"Why does she call you da? Savannah's grandmother asked. It was strange saying grandmother she couldn't be more than forty-two.

"Because we are her family. Do you realize she would have lasted only a couple of days if we hadn't found her? She is our child, and we love her more than anything in this world. We are going to give all of you a chance to grieve your son. Here is our address. Come visit us when you are ready, and you can get to know Savannah. This would be too much for her right now. We came here because she is your granddaughter, and we thought you would like to know her."

I wanted to get the hell out of there before they decided

to take Savannah right then and scare her to death. We returned to the vehicle, returned to the hotel, and left from there. I looked over at Charlie, and I thought she might cry at any moment. Savannah was sleeping, and Charlie leaned back with her eyes closed.

Now, we would be waiting for them to show up at our house to take our baby from us. I should have ripped those papers to shreds.

"They didn't know Gregory was dead all this time. Did Savannah's mother not inform them? The people who ran her out of the town must have made her stay there, and I bet you anything she died by starvation. She must have given what little they would get from her family to the baby," I glanced at Charlie as she spoke, surprised at how angry she was.

"We'll never know how she died or how Gregory died unless the Scotts bring those bodies here; then, they would know what happened to both of them," I mused aloud.

"Can they do that?" Charlie asked.

"Yes," Ghost affirmed before I could respond.

"I want to bring those kids back here to be buried."

"Charlie, this isn't cheap; it could cost a lot of money," Ghost explained.

"I'm willing to bear the cost. I want to bring Savannah's parents' home for burial. What's the next step?" Charlie declared.

"I'll handle it. I'll fly over and show them where they are buried," Ghost volunteered.

"Thank you. I will let his family know what we are going to do and see if they have a family plot they want them in," she turned and looked at me. "What do we do if they try to take Savannah from us?"

"Let's cross that bridge when we come to it."

23

CHARLIE

I'VE BEEN WORRIED THAT SAVANNAH'S OTHER FAMILY MIGHT show up with the law and try to take Savannah from us. If they do, they'll have a fight on their hands. I heard my phone ringing and picked it up. "Hello."

"Hey, Charlie, it's Marcus. Thought you and Steel should know someone's looking into you two. Any idea who?"

"I'm sure it's Savannah's other relatives. We reached out to them about their son and told them about him; they didn't know he had died, so now they know about Savannah. They're probably checking us out," I replied.

"Do they want to take her from you?" Marcus inquired.

"I'm not sure. We'll have to wait and see. I'm surprised we haven't seen them yet. We've invited them to visit their granddaughter. I'm bringing Gregory and his wife's bodies from Sudan for burial in the family plot. They're probably busy with arrangements," I explained.

"That's generous of you."

"They're Savannah's birth parents; they deserve to rest where they can be visited by loved ones. So, about moving here—"

"I need to sort out some things first, especially with Jaz. Once that's done, I'll consider it," Marcus interjected. "I want to make sure none of the FBI stuff follows me where I go."

"I understand. Get that all sorted out, and we'll see you when we see you," I chose not to mention that Jaz had been putting on weight; she hasn't said anything about it. So all of us on the mountain are waiting for her to tell us her happy news. We just ignore that she's getting bigger.

I noticed Sara wagging her tail, at the same time I heard Steel conversing with Spike and Mertle. Opening the door, I was surprised to see Ghost with them. I wondered if he had managed to retrieve Gregory and his wife's bodies.

"Everything is taken care of. Gregory's family just wants a private funeral," Ghost reported. They might visit next Saturday if that's alright, with you and Steel."

"They want to visit. Do you think they'll demand custody of Savannah? I can't allow them to take our daughter. If I have to take her away, I will," I said, frowning.

"I think they just want to meet her," Ghost reassured.

"Sweetheart, let's wait and see how things unfold before we worry about running away with Savannah," Steel advised, wrapping his arm around me. "Ghost, care for a beer?"

"I'd love one," Ghost accepted, following Steel inside.

"I think I'll sit out here for a while," I said.

"Do you want us to come back out and sit with you?" Steel asked.

"No need, I'm good," I said as I walked onto the grass. I lay down on the cool grass, joined by Sara, Spike, and Mertle. I was in deep meditation when I felt a presence beside me. Turning my head, I saw Allison lying on the grass beside me.

"What are you doing?" I asked softly.

"You're not the only one who likes to meditate," she replied quietly.

"Need to clear your head?" I whispered.

"Yes," she whispered back.

"Do you want to talk about it?" I asked.

"Maybe later."

We lay in silence until Savannah plopped onto me. Smiling, I hugged her close. Turning, I noticed Steel and Ghost watching us. Ghost's gaze lingered on Allison. They both needed to move forward from the past.

As Ghost walked away, I joined Steel, who embraced me. We watched Savannah sit on Allison and kiss her. Allison laughed as she hugged Savannah to her.

"Allison, stay for dinner; I'm cooking hamburgers. Viper, Bailey, and the kids will be here," Steel called out.

"I would love to stay for dinner. Thank you!" She picked Savannah up and followed us into the house. We walked into the kitchen, and I made a quick salad while Steel made the burgers. Then, we carried all the makings out to the grill. Viper, Bailey, and the little ones joined us.

"Tell us what's going on with you," Viper prompted his sister Allison.

"You all don't need to hear my problems," she said glancing at her brother, Viper.

"Tell us; it'll get our minds on something else," I said, watching Allison.

"I'm moving away," Allison disclosed.

"What? Why?" Viper exclaimed. "You can't move away. No, this mountain is our family's legacy. Why would you move away?"

"I need a change. I'm thirty-three, and I have no life. I can't keep dwelling on Ghost," Allison tried explaining. "It's not getting better. It's the same every day. I want a life, and if I move away, maybe I can find someone. We don't have to love each other. We could be friends. I don't even go on dates because everyone here knows Ghost."

"Why are the two of you not together?" I asked, curious but not wanting to be nosy. "It's so apparent to anyone you love him, and he loves you."

"We are not together because James Bellmont strayed. That's right, I thought he was happy with me. He said he loved me and wanted us to be together forever, but he lied. He didn't love me enough because he strayed when I was away at medical school."

"Are you sure he strayed? That doesn't sound like something Ghost would do. Did someone tell you this?" I asked because now I was nosy.

"Yes, I am damn sure! I got the weekend off and decided to surprise him. When I went to his room, he was lying naked in bed with a woman who was as naked as he was. I woke him up and demanded to know what was going on. We were engaged; we were getting married in two weeks."

Allison pinched the bridge of her nose, and I knew she didn't want to cry. "You sound like everyone on this mountain, and I would have thought the same thing if I hadn't seen them myself."

"What did he say about it?"

"He said he didn't know who she was or how she got in his bed. He was at the bar celebrating Knox getting into the Delta Force Recon Marines, and Levi dropped him off at his house where he was alone."

"Wow, what a pickle he got himself into."

"Exactly, and I'm so frigging pitiful that I've still wanted to be near him, still after all this time. Call me stupid. I opened my eyes and realized what I was doing: moping around this place. So, I start my new job at the hospital on the first of the month. I found an apartment until I decide if I want to buy my own place."

I knew Viper wasn't happy about his sister's decision. "I think you're making a mistake. What about the mountain folk who won't go to any other doctor, the older ones who will only see you?" Viper asked.

"They'll manage like they always do, and it's not like I'll be that far away. I'll be an hour away, close enough to see my family when I want to visit."

"But you'll be working in a hospital; you'll be stuck inside all day. I know you are not going to like that."

"I'll adjust. Other people work inside buildings and manage just fine," Allison said, taking a bite from her hamburger.

"Those other people are not you. I'm sorry. I'm supposed to be excited and happy for you, and all I'm thinking about are the rest of us missing you," Viper said, looking sad. "You still have to come to Sunday dinners once in a while. And the family reunion, you can't miss that."

"I would never miss that. You'll never know I'm gone. I promise you'll see me all the time."

"You're our only sister, so have you told Ryan and the others?"

"No, I'll tell them tonight," Allison said.

I glanced at Viper; I knew he didn't like his only sister leaving the mountain. I also wondered what Ghost would say about Allison moving away, even if it was only an hour's drive from here.

24

STEEL

I couldn't understand why Ghost reacted so strongly to Allison leaving the mountain. It was as if I had told him she moved to the other side of the moon. He punched a hole in my wall and stormed out without a word.

"Did he at least say where he was going?" Spartan asked, concern etched in his expression.

"No, just that he's taking off and might be gone for a year or so," I replied, frustration evident in my tone.

"A year. What's gotten into him? All because Allison Reed has moved off the mountain. I always wondered, between the two of us, why he didn't force her to listen to him. I've told him time after time to kidnap her and make her listen to him. But he wouldn't do anything; it was like they walked on thin ice around each other. I'll see you later," Spartan said.

Charlie walked out onto the porch, looking like her world had just caved in. "What's wrong?" I asked, dreading the answer.

"The Scotts called and said they wanted to visit us on Saturday, and they'll be here at nine."

"Good, let's clear the air. I was getting tired of waiting around for them to call us. But don't stress about it, sweetheart. God put us in the right spot at the right time to save Savannah. She's our daughter, and that won't change."

"Steel, I'm naturally a worrier. You should know that by now. I'm trying to change, and I will, but it'll take time," Charlie replied. I thought she would say something else, but then she changed her mind.

"How about not wearing your gun on Saturday?"

"You don't understand what would happen if I didn't carry my gun on a day that some lunatic showed up with a machine gun," Charlie replied.

"Sweetheart, I'm here to take care of you and Savannah; you don't have to wear your gun every day."

"Steel, I can take care of myself. I know there have been a few times that I haven't been able to do thaAt, and that's when you can step in and take care of me. But I am a homicide detective and know what happens in this world where danger lurks around every corner. I'll think about not wearing my gun on the Saturday they come to visit," Charlie said. I was glad she decided to at least think about it.

"That's all I ask. At least they won't think we are overly paranoid. I have to talk to Viper and see if Ghost said anything to him about where he was going. I can't believe he just left without saying something to me."

"Savannah and I are walking over to visit with Grandma Molly and Aunt Hillary. Oh, here comes Jaz. Maybe she wants to walk with us."

"Has she mentioned anything about having a baby? Or are we still not saying anything?"

"We won't say anything until she brings it up first, and then we can say how excited we are for her," Charlie said walking to meet Jaz and the boys. I waved to Jaz and then turned to walk to Viper and Bailey's home.

∼

"I can't believe Ghost just up and left. He must have said something," frustration evident in Viper's tone.

Viper was as surprised as I was that Ghost would take off the way he did. "Yeah, he did. He said, 'I'm tired of waiting for her to forgive me for something I didn't do,'" I recounted. "So I guess I can tell Allison that Ghost is gone and see what she thinks about it."

"He should have settled this when it happened instead of letting it eat away at Allison like a damn cancer. Both of them are equally to blame. My sister has missed out on life because of their stubbornness," Viper said, and then he sighed. "It's really sad, I should have made them confront this years ago."

I shook my head, trying to make sense of it all. "And what about that incident with Allison finding him in bed with another woman? Ghost swears he's innocent, and I believe him. He's loved Allison for years and wouldn't jeopardize their relationship. But who was she? Ghost mentioned she ran off as soon as Allison caught them. Do you think someone hired her to sabotage their relationship?"

"We've discussed this over and over, even in that Iranian prison. Weston thinks someone might have been behind it. He suggested Ghost revisit anyone who might have had a grudge against them. I forgot to mention it to Ghost. What's on your mind besides Ghost?" Viper asked, taking a long drink from his beer.

"Savannah's family from Georgia is visiting next Saturday. Charlie worries they will try to take Savannah from us. I'll be honest, Viper, that thought scares me too. I don't know what I would do if they tried to separate her from us."

"Do you have any reason to think they'd do that?" Viper inquired, concern in his eyes.

"No, but I know if it were my granddaughter, I'd fight tooth and nail to keep her. I just hope they'll see how happy Savannah is with us and how much we love her."

"You'll have to make them understand. Show them how much you love her and she loves you. Do you need a beer?"

"Sure, I have time for a beer. Charlie and Savannah went to visit Miss Molly and Miss Hillary. We have a big job coming up next week. I hate to leave Charlie with all of this going on, but I have a job to do."

25

CHARLIE

I opened the door before they could knock; I smiled and invited Savannah's other family inside. I heard Savannah as she came running into the room, followed by Steel. She was laughing and ran to where I stood. I scooped her up and turned her so her grandparents could see her.

"She's beautiful. Hello Savannah. Can I hold her?" her grandmother asked eagerly.

"Of course," I replied, though inwardly my nerves were on edge. Handing Savannah over, I suggested we all move to the family room.

Bailey emerged from the kitchen, offering iced tea. Relief washed over me at the sight of her. "Let me take care of that," I volunteered, jumping up.

"I have all the snacks here," Jaz said, walking from the kitchen. "Should I put them outside, or will we be in here?" I could have cried when my friends showed up to help me through this heartbreaking ordeal.

"Why don't we let Sherry and Gray spend time with Savannah, and then we'll go out and have something to eat," Steel said, smiling at Bailey and Jaz.

Savannah spotted Jaz's twins outside, eager to play. I intervened gently. "Savannah, sweetheart, you can play later. Grandma..." I stopped talking and smiled at Sherry. "It feels strange calling you two grandma and grandpa. How about we pick names like Meme and Pop?"

"That sounds perfect to me. I like the name Meme. What about you, Pop?" Sherry said, laughing.

"I prefer that name to Grandpa. Are there always kids here playing outside?"

"This has always been the go-to house, even when my grandparents lived here. There are plenty of Petersons on this mountain," Steel explained, running a hand through his hair. "We want you to know how much we love Savannah. She's our baby; from the moment I saw her standing alone in that hot desert, I knew God put me there for a reason. And that reason was Savannah. If you plan to take her away from us, you'll have a fight on your hands."

"We were actually going to discuss that with you. We would love for Savannah to live with us. She's all we have left of our son. We know you didn't have to contact us, but because you're good people, you didn't hesitate to let us know we had a granddaughter. However, Sherry has cancer, and she starts chemotherapy tomorrow, so there's no way we'd be able to care for her right now," Jim explained, wiping his eyes.

"I'm so sorry you're going through this," I said, rising to embrace Sherry. "Tell me how I can help?" Savannah, seeing me hug Sherry, she kissed Sherry on the cheek.

"Will you promise me that we'll get to visit Savannah often? I know we live in another state, and it can be expensive to travel back and forth, but I need to see her as much as possible," Sherry pleaded.

"Are you saying we get to keep our baby?" I felt my heart racing.

"We could see how much you two loved Savannah. I never want our granddaughter to think we didn't want her. We love her so much, and I know you do too. So yes, we are letting Savannah stay here with her mother and father," Sherry replied. I stepped out of the room to collect myself. I have never been so happy in my life—strong arms enveloped me, and turning I wrapped my arms around him and held him too. "We get to keep her," I whispered.

"Yes, sweetheart and our baby looked a little anxious when you left the room," Steel took my hand, and we returned to our guests. I smiled in surprise when I saw the youngest boy holding Savannah, and she was talking as fast as she could. Even though he couldn't understand her, he agreed with every word she said.

"I have my own plane, so the cost of the visits won't be an issue. I'll take care of all the trips," I said, reaching for Savannah. I needed to hold her to me, just to reassure me that she was mine.

"You have your own plane; I thought you were a Homicide Detective?" Gray remarked in surprise.

"I was, but I'm also an inventor, so I have a plane. We'll be visiting you often," I explained.

"Why did you call him Steel?" Sherry interjected.

"That's Levi's Delta Force name, and everyone calls him Steel," I clarified. "Why don't we go outside? It's a beautiful day," Jaz suggested, handing Gray a piece of paper. "This recipe was my grandmother's; it was passed down in her family who were Native Indians. She used this recipe when she was given a few months to live because she had cancer. She lived another thirty years. You need to make it fresh every day."

Gray accepted the recipe gratefully, promising to follow it diligently.

"You have to use fresh fruit and always eat only fresh food, stay away from meat of any kind. While you are drinking this juice, because this drink will clear your entire body of the bad cancer. Even if you don't believe in this drink do it anyway," Jaz said.

"Thank you, should I drink it in the mornings?"

"My grandma said she drank it in the morning and sometimes if she felt like she needed another boost she would drink another one," Steel said, as he took Savannah, and we followed him outside where some kids played basketball.

"Who are these kids?" Gray asked, looking around. He could see other homes and parts of the town further down the hill.

"They live on the mountain. Most of them are Petersons, so as you can see, Savannah has lots of family members. Now, we're your family too, so feel free to visit whenever you want. Our home is spacious, with plenty of room for everyone," I assured them.

"That's very kind of you. Thank you, we will take you up on that offer. The kids are having a great time."

Bailey and Jaz set out snacks on the table then we sat down and enjoyed our visit. Every time I glanced at Steel, I knew he would not let Savannah out of his sight, and neither would I. We have our baby and we get to keep her forever. Of course, I will have some legal documents drawn up for the Scotts to sign, to ensure no one would ever try to take her from us.

26

STEEL

I felt a sense of relief wash over me now that we no longer had to worry about our daughter being taken from us. I was on my way to Afghanistan to bring some Americans home. It's astonishing to think that there are still hundreds of Americans stranded there, awaiting evacuation.

I glanced around at the guys pouring over the details of the five individuals we were tasked with rescuing. I noted the difference of finally having our own aircraft for transportation, eliminating the need to rely on borrowed planes from friends.

All of the people were from the same family: a mother, three children, and her mother who came over for a visit and got stuck here when the Marines withdrew from Afghanistan. They were lucky that they were staying with someone in a remote area and had remained relatively undisturbed until recently when the Taliban began targeting homes in search of Americans.

Our plan involved landing at a border airstrip where a waiting vehicle awaited us. I fervently hoped it would be spacious enough for everyone. Accompanying me on this mission were Spartan, Rebel, and Reaper, all cousins to Ghost, who was still missing in action.

As Spartan piloted the plane, his demeanor suggested he was preoccupied, perhaps with the mysterious calls he had been receiving. Though the calls had ceased for a while, the possibility of danger lingered. He mentioned investigating who might harbor enough animosity towards him to wish him harm.

As we started landing, it was late at night. We planned to do most of our traveling late at night, so we were less likely to be noticed. I hoped we were in and out quickly; the last thing we wanted was to get stuck over here. I didn't see a vehicle anywhere as we got off the plane. We were walking when a bus came barreling toward us.

We all took cover until we heard laughing, and I smiled when I heard Gideon Oswald laugh; the last time I saw him was when we saved him and his boys. His wife had just been murdered, and Gideon, who is also known as Raider, his Delta Force name, had killed four of the men who killed his wife. He was a little crazy when Cheryl was murdered in front of him. I wondered what he was doing here. He was raised on the mountain like the rest of us but hasn't lived there in years.

"What are you doing here?" I asked.

"I've decided to join the team. Since I was here and knew you were on your way, I agreed to bring the bus. Where are we going?"

"I'm happy you were able to join us. Where are the boys?"

"They're with my Dad. I heard you got yourself a wife, and I believe Benni told me she was none other than Charlotte Primrose Randal."

Spartan interrupted, stepping in front of me. "Where did you see Benni?"

"I saw her when the boys and I were in Spain; she has a home there. She runs that Digital Magazine from Spain, focusing on the Appalachian Mountains and its residents," Raider explained.

"What the hell does she know about our mountain? She's been gone for three years and hasn't come home in all that time," Spartan said angrily. He and Benni have always had a thing, but Spartan wouldn't admit that he had feelings for Benni.

"She's there at least once a month; she visits all over the mountain when she is there. Haven't you seen her at all?"

"No, she must time her visits when I'm away. Why the hell does she live in Spain? Her family is still on the mountain," Spartan declared.

"I can't answer that question. Although I think Benni takes most of them with her when she returns to Spain," I replied, glancing at the road we traveled down. "What do you think about this rescue," I asked Raider.

"It's going to be tight. The Taliban has ramped up their efforts to hunt down Americans, aiming to extort ransom from their families. And unfortunately, their treatment of captives is brutal, especially towards women. They harbor a deep-seated hatred for all Americans," Raider explained.

"We'll proceed cautiously; I see something ahead," Raider announced as he veered off the main road onto a side route, opting to turn off the headlights in case someone spotted us.

"What side of the border are we on?" I asked, taking out my night binoculars.

"It doesn't matter much. The Taliban disregard borders

when it suits them, and no one intervenes as long as they don't stray too far," Raider replied, emphasizing the volatile nature of the region.

I watched the vehicle drawing closer, with these night vision goggles, I could see almost anything at night. They veered away I surmised they were just someone on their way home. We kept driving until we spotted the glow of distant lights, indicating homes were scattered about the area.

We took our time driving; we wanted to avoid drawing unwanted attention. "Where are we supposed to pick up the family?" I inquired the closer we got to the houses. "Who the hell is that?" I said as a jeep came barreling toward us.

"Get down!" Raider bellowed as bullets struck our bus, shattering glass everywhere, prompting us to seek cover. Raider pulled off the road, and we had our guns out when we saw the jeep turn with no headlights. We all had our night goggles on and could see them slowing down.

Allowing them to draw closer, I fired my gun, causing the driver to fall out of the jeep, and the other guy started firing his weapon as the jeep went off the road. Spartan fired his weapon and shot the other guy.

"How did they discover our location? Only Jeramy Stone, the man who hired us to rescue his family, knew our destination," I pondered aloud.

"I vetted Stone; his story checked out. He was even on the television talking about his family and begging the government to bring his family home. He even paid upfront," Rebel responded.

"Something isn't adding up. What did Stone say when you talked to him? Who talked to him?"

"I spoke to him," Rebel interjected. "He seemed genuine. He mentioned only one of us should be coming here in case we came upon trouble. He specifically requested Spartan, citing his reputation for swift maneuvering, he said he had heard stories about Spartan. It struck me as odd, but he became emotional when discussing his family."

"Fuck, we need to find out who's behind the threat on Spartan's life," I exclaimed, glancing around at Spartan. "Any idea whose wife you might have crossed paths with?"

"I haven't slept with anyone's wife, and you damn well know I wouldn't stoop to that," Spartan retorted firmly.

"Have you been able to think of any other enemies you might have?" I pressed.

"No, but I'll damn sure find out if I have any enemies. Let's go home since we were sent on a bogus rescue," Spartan declared, rising to his feet and walking away.

"Regardless of the deception, that family still needs our help. Who's up for doing a good deed today?" I rallied my team.

"Do we know their location?" Rebel inquired.

"I can find out in no time," I replied, retrieving my phone. I called a couple of people and had the address a moment later. "The house is thirty miles from the border, and we've already covered at least ten. How about we take this family home where they belong?"

"Let's do it," Spartan affirmed as he returned to where we were. We cleared the bus of shattered glass and got back in and followed the directions that were provided. It took seven frigging hours before we found the house.

I knocked on the door, and it creaked open slightly. "I'm here to take your family back home. We'll give them ten minutes to gather your belongings before we depart," I announced. The door swung wide, and before I knew it, the woman who answered had pulled me inside.

"Who sent you?" she demanded.

"That will take too long to explain. Are you Jeramy's wife?" I asked.

"Yes," she sobbed.

"Then gather your mother and your kids. You're going home," I instructed.

"Mama, kids, let's go. We're going home," she called out. I stood back as the room was filled with kids and an elderly woman was crying. They rushed outside and boarded the bus without grabbing anything.

"Be careful; we don't want any glass getting in your eyes," I cautioned, glancing at the youngest child, who appeared to be around twelve or thirteen.

"How did the windows break?" he inquired.

"They were shot out," I replied.

"That's why I'll be glad to get home. I never want to come back here. Some kids I knew got shot for no reason. We've been here too long. Did my Dad send you to get us?" he asked anxiously.

"Yes, your father sent us," I assured him, deciding to keep the explanation simple. I made a mental note to inform his father as soon as possible.

"We haven't had a full night's sleep since the Taliban took over, so if we all fall asleep, don't think anything about it. We are just tired."

"You go ahead and sleep; we'll wake you when we get home," I said, smiling at the grandmother.

I called the father, who cried while on the phone. He said he gave all their savings to someone who said they would bring his family home. I explained that we told the family that he sent us to get them, and he was so grateful that he promised to pray for all of us every night.

When we landed our plane in America, he was there to greet them. Even while everyone was crying, he came over, hugged all of us, and kissed our cheeks. "I can never repay you; I will pray for all of you every night," he explained as his family hung onto him.

27

CHARLIE

I watched Jaz walk up the steps; she was ready to have her baby anytime now. Savannah played with the boys as she sat down.

"When do you plan on breaking the news about the baby?" I inquired, a smile on my face.

She wiped away a tear, "I wanted to tell Marcus first. I should have told him when that awful man took my son, but he left before I had a chance to say anything. Do you know what happened to that man?"

"No, it's better if we say nothing about him. Marcus took care of everything. How are you feeling?" I asked, concerned.

"I'm feeling fine physically, but emotionally, I'm lonesome for Marcus; the baby will be here in a week or two. I thought for sure he would be here by now. Have you spoken to him?" Jaz inquired.

"No, I haven't talked to him. Do you know what you are having?"

"No, I wanted Marcus here when we found out. Now, I'll

wait until the baby is here. The boys want a sister just like Savannah, whom they adore," Jaz explained.

"She is the best baby in the world. Of course, I'm her mother, so I might be a little biased as a mother would be," I said, grinning.

"How is Sherry doing?"

"She's doing remarkably well; her cancer is in remission. I hope it stays that way. They're such wonderful people, and I'm glad we told them about Savannah," I replied.

"Ouch, that was sharp."

"Are you in labor?" I asked, standing up to hurry to her.

"No, I still have a couple of weeks left. It can't be labor. I'm waiting for Marcus. It's just a small cramp. I've been having them on and off all morning," she reassured.

"I'm calling Steel; he's at Jacob's house," I said, grabbing my phone and dialing Steel's number. He promised to come home right away.

Jacob was with him when he pulled into the driveway. "Are you in a lot of pain?" Steel inquired worriedly.

"No, Charlie's just being overcautious. I'm not in labor," Jaz insisted.

"Then why the hell did you grab your stomach and wince?" Jacob pressed.

Jacob paced anxiously, "I am not delivering my sister's baby. Let's go to the hospital."

"No, I'm not having this baby until Marcus arrives," Jaz declared, stomping her foot and wincing again.

"Is Marcus on his way?" Steel asked.

"No, I can't have the baby yet," Jaz replied tearfully.

"Okay, this is what we are going to do; the kids can stay here with Jacob; we are going to the hospital," Steel said as he stood. "Do you want Mom there with you?"

"I'm not going until Marcus is here," Jaz said, as a fat tear ran down her face. All of us looked at each other when a vehicle pulled into the driveway on the other side of the house.

"Did you call the ambulance," Jaz accused, looking at Jacob.

"No," he said. That's when Marcus walked around the corner of the house.

"Why are you crying, sweetheart?" what did you say to her? he demanded to know, looking at Steel.

"I didn't say anything," Steel said with a grin, diverting Marcus's attention back to Jaz, who was still in tears.

Marcus took her hand and helped her to her feet, wrapping her in his embrace before stepping back to look at her. "You should have called me," he gently scolded, placing his hand on her stomach, and kissing it.

"Marcus, I'm in labor. We don't have time to make it to the hospital. I'll have the baby here. Can you help me inside?" Jaz pleaded.

Marcus scooped her up and carried her to a spare room at the back of the house. He kissed her passionately, before laying her on the bed. I turned to Steel and Jacob.

"You two can watch the kids. I'll help Marcus with the delivery," I said, masking my nerves.

"Does he know what he's doing?" Jacob asked, nervously.

"Yes, he's delivered many babies. Now go check on Savannah and the twins," I instructed. Deep down, I prayed everything would go smoothly.

"Charlie, I can't believe you didn't call me. The woman I love is having my child, and you said nothing," Marcus exclaimed incredulously.

"That's because Jaz never mentioned anything to us; we all pretended not to acknowledge how much she was progressing. We understood she was waiting for you; who could have predicted you'd take this long," I responded, stealing a glance at Jaz, who wore a grin.

"Hey, sweetheart, don't worry. I've got this under control," Marcus reassured her.

"I'm not worried. Are you staying this time?" Jaz inquired.

"Yes, I am. I bought Aunt Hillary and Aunt Molly's house; they'll be living with us. We'll get married as soon as possible. How about we have Viper marry us?" Marcus proposed.

"Yes! Call him, Charlie," Jaz eagerly agreed.

"Right now? While you're in labor?" I asked.

"Yes, please," Jaz replied, her gaze on Marcus.

I shook my head, apprehensive about the idea, but I dialed Viper nonetheless. When I heard a noise behind me, I turned to find him there.

"I was outside," He explained. Baily and Izzy entered the room, followed by Steel, Savannah, and the boys, who rushed to Marcus. That was the quickest ceremony I've ever witnessed, but there wasn't a dry eye in the house. When we turned to leave, Jaz's parents stood there, tears streaming down their faces.

"Everyone out," Marcus ordered when Jaz experienced another intense pain. "Izzy, you can stay since you have more experience."

"Is mommy having our sister now?" Caleb asked.

"Yes, but we don't know if the baby is a girl yet," I clarified.

"We know she's a girl," Cruise, the other twin, declared before they darted outside, while we sat in the family room waiting for news of the baby.

Thirty minutes later, Izzy emerged with a beautiful baby

girl, adorned with the Peterson family's striking silver eyes and Marcus's black hair. What a day, and it wasn't even noon.

"Who's hungry for lunch," I asked, surveying the room.

"I'll help you in the kitchen," Bailey offered, rising from her seat. She chuckled as we made our way to the kitchen. "You should have seen Viper, eyeing me like I was going to go into labor any minute."

"When's your baby due? I thought it was last week," I inquired.

"The Thursday, but he's not ready yet. He'll make his entrance when he's good and ready. I admit, I'm quite anxious for this one to arrive. He's larger than the others, so I'm not taking any chances; I'll be at the hospital at the first sign of labor," Bailey confessed, a hint of nervousness in her voice.

"I'm just grateful Izzy was in there and not me. I'm sure I would've fainted and embarrassed myself." I admitted.

"No, you wouldn't have. You're one of the strongest women I know," Bailey complimented me.

Touched by her words, a tear escaped my eye, and I embraced her.

After the ambulance whisked Jaz off to the hospital, Marcus took the boys with him to the hospital. He wanted them to be involved in every aspect of welcoming their little sister. Marcus mentioned they both cried tears of joy upon learning they had a sister.

Despite feeling a pang in my heart for never experiencing pregnancy myself, I couldn't help but marvel at Bailey's description of it being a magical sensation when the baby first moves. She even let me feel her baby's movements, confirming her words. Indeed, it was magical.

28

STEEL

I heard a noise and glanced over my shoulder to see Ghost stepping onto the porch. It had been eight months since he'd been gone.

"It's about damn time. How are you doing?" I asked.

"I'm good. It feels great being home. I let my emotions take over for a while, but I'm over all that emotional crap now. No more for me. You can send me away as soon as you get a job. I'm ready to return to what's normal," Ghost replied.

I smiled. "Where have you been?"

"I walked through a few jungles on this wild journey with some crazy dudes I met up with. When I realized these men didn't care if they lived or died, I went off on my own and got lost. I ended up in this village that has only seen a handful of people like me. I've been there for the last three months. My mind's much more relaxed than it's been for the last five years."

"Good, I'm glad that is all taken care of. We have something coming up in a couple of weeks. It's not big. When they are out of school, we take a couple of kids to their grandparents who live in another country."

"That sounds great; let me know when I need to leave. How is everyone else doing?" Ghost inquired.

I knew he was asking about Allison, "Everyone is doing fine. Jaz had her baby, she and Marcus were married, and he bought the Randal sisters' home. They get to stay there and live with Marcus and Jaz.

"Bailey and Viper had a baby boy. Savannah is growing too fast, and Allison is doing okay," I updated him.

He nodded and stood up to leave. "Come to dinner tonight; Savannah will be happy to see you."

"Thanks, but my grandfather has already cornered me about dinner. He also volunteered me to cook it."

"How is your grandpa doing? I haven't seen him out and about lately," I asked.

"He's been taking care of his wife, Adeline. She had a fall and broke her hip. He hunted me down and asked me to come home. I was already on my way, but I hurried when he called. You know he has loved her since he was a young man, and they didn't see each other again until a few years ago. Carrie has been staying there and helping him."

"Are you worried about him?" I asked.

"I am. Gramp's health has gone down a lot; I was surprised when I saw him. I know he's eighty-seven, but he's always been healthy and strong. I think it's taken a toll on him taking care of Adeline. He raised Carrie, me, and my cousins after our parents all died in that accident. I love him like he was my father, mother, and grandfather all in one," Ghost said, running his hand through his hair.

"I know, but remember he may be tired; the only thing you can do is be there for him."

"It's good to see you again, Steel; I always feel better after talking to you. You should have been a therapist," Ghost said, walking away grinning.

I chuckled, remembering how everyone used to tell me that years ago when they weren't interested in my advice. They would always say I should have been a therapist and let people who pay money get my advice.

"Was that Ghost leaving?" Charlie asked as she wrapped her arms around me.

"Yes, he's back to stay. His grandfather is getting up there in age, and of course, he's worried about him and his wife Adeline. Is Savannah napping?" I asked as I leaned down and kissed her.

"Yes, she wore herself out playing today."

"Maybe we can slip into bed for an hour or so," I suggested. For an answer, Charlie pulled me into the house and our room. We undressed each other and fell on the bed laughing. We had made love all night last night; I could never get enough of Charlie. I loved her so much; my life was perfect. We were there for thirty minutes when we heard someone in the house.

"Did we lock the door?" Charlie asked.

"No," we always had to lock the door at our house if we were going to our room in the daytime because people always came and went. "Hurry, get dressed before they come back here," she said, trying not to laugh.

I pulled on my pants and shirt and left the room as Charlie got into the shower. Spartan was taking out stuff for a roast beef sandwich.

"Do you want one?" he asked.

"Yeah, I'll take one," I started getting other stuff out. If I was going to have a sandwich, I wanted everything on it. "What's on your mind?"

"I received a message today, and it was on the front seat

of my truck. It said, 'Are you even wondering who's sending you to all those places? I looked at the outdoor cameras, and I didn't see anything on any of them. How could someone put a message in my truck without me seeing anything on the camera?" Spartan recounted.

"I don't know. Do you think it's someone from around here?" I asked.

"When I find out who it is, I'm going to kill him I don't care if I go to prison, but he's dead," Spartan declared.

"How do you know it's a 'him'? Maybe it's a woman who is angry with you. Can you think of any woman who might hold a grudge against you? Perhaps someone you turned down," I suggested.

"I'm always turning women down, but I can't think of anyone who'd know how to orchestrate trips to other countries. I just wanted to give you a heads-up in case you notice any strangers around. I've already alerted the others," Spartan said.

"We'll have to catch this bastard before they escalate beyond sending you places and leaving messages. Individuals like this tend to only get worse, and now that they've sent you a message, it shows they're serious about whatever they're planning. What kind of paper was used?" I inquired.

"They used a piece of brown paper bag and wrote with a crayon. I'm having it checked for fingerprints," Spartan replied.

"Do you think he might have children, and that's where the crayon came from?" I mused.

"I hope not because they're going to die," Spartan said, as he stood. "I'll catch you later."

"Yeah, I'll see you later. Let me know if you hear anything else," I replied, accompanying Spartan to the door.

"Who was here?" Charlie asked as I was cleaning up our sandwich fixings.

"Spartan. Remember me telling you about someone sending Spartan all over, even to another country," I reminded her.

"Yes."

"Well, today, he had a message on his front seat. The cameras around their home didn't catch anyone near his vehicle. The person used a brown paper bag and a crayon," I explained.

"What kind of paper bag? Was it the thin kind from a drug store or the thick kind from a grocery store?" Charlie inquired.

"Does it matter?" I asked.

"I think if he was in his vehicle when writing it, he might have had a prescription bag in there; he grabbed a crayon from the floor of his car and wrote the note. But I'm sure he had on gloves. He probably bought those in the pharmacy, where he picked up his medicine," Charlie theorized as she made herself a sandwich.

"That actually sounds like it makes sense," I conceded, joining her at the table.

"Of course, it does. I've tracked down people like this before," Charlie said confidently.

"Do you think it's a man?" I probed.

"Yes, a woman, no matter how rushed she was, would likely prefer using nicer the paper and pen to be nice, especially for someone as handsome as Spartan.

"You think Spartan is handsome?" I chuckled.

"Sure, don't you?" Charlie shot back, smiling.

"I never really thought about it," I admitted with a smile.

"He's not as good-looking as you are, but all of you Delta

Force men are attractive. I'm surprised all of you aren't married," Charlie remarked.

"Some are too stubborn; others haven't fallen in love. I never loved anyone until you came into my life. Maybe you can assist us with some work from time to time," I suggested.

"Really, I'd love to help out whenever you need me. I love being with Savannah, but it would be nice to engage my brain every now and then. If I could look at that piece of paper, I'd love that. My heart is racing just thinking about getting back into detective work. Not that I wouldn't want to do anything, but you know what I mean. I wouldn't change being a mother for anything. I love my baby and taking care of her, but I did love working on solving crimes," Charlie said, explaining her feelings.

"Sweetheart, why didn't you say something earlier? Of course, you want to do something else. I'll speak to the guys, and you can help investigate some of our cases. You've already solved a few for us. Are you getting bored?" I asked. "I should have realized you'd need more excitement."

"Take a deep breath, honey; I'm not bored at all. I don't have time to be bored. After all, I'm living in the house where the Peterson King resides, which makes me the go-to person for every Peterson. It's no wonder you're always dispensing advice. It's how you were raised," Charlie reassured me.

"I wouldn't say I was a King, but I did get pushed into hearing from everyone after my grandparents left me this home. I have to admit I loved it, and I still do, I think, it's because I felt needed," I reflected. "I took over the family reunion every year and kept doing Sunday dinners once a month. I never even asked if you minded any of that."

"I love it. I'm not a very good cook, but everyone already

knows that, so I get assigned to making the fruit salad," she chuckled. "I love your family. The best thing that ever happened to me was Grandma Molly pushing my wheelchair down the hill. I have my beautiful baby girl and a man I love more than anything in this world."

"Are we going back to bed?" I asked.

I heard that sexy chuckle as she stood. "No, Savannah is waking up," Charlie said as she bent and kissed me. I couldn't help but pull her onto my lap, and our kiss grew passionate. It was always like this with us. We couldn't keep our hands off each other.

29

STEEL

I sat on the porch watching Charlie push Savannah on the swing set jungle gym she fell in love with at Costco. Seeing her excitement was priceless. Assembling it, however, was another story. I had my Delta Force team here to help me sort out the parts, so we would know what to do. It was like constructing a house.

I spotted Spartan making his way up the mountain and wondered if he had made any headway in figuring out who was out to get him.

"How are you holding up?" I greeted him.

"I'm good. Ghost and Rebel are taking the kids to their grandparents, and Ghost seemed like he was on the verge of pulling his hair out. It's odd how he completely lost it when Allison moved off the mountain. What's up with him? It's time he moved on with his life; I mentioned that to him last week," Spartan remarked, rubbing his chest.

"How did he react?" I inquired.

"He pushed me off the hill, and I ended up in the swimming hole. By the time I got out, he was gone. Grandpa's wife, Adeline, is back in the hospital," Spartan ran his hand through his hair. "They put Gramp's a bed in there because he had been sitting on that damn chair all night. We're worried because the doctor said she won't be coming home. I reckon Gramps won't last long after she's gone. I don't know what to do," Spartan said, glancing at me.

"All you can do is be there for him," I reassured him.

"Yeah, that's all we can do. Allison has been checking on him during the day. She'll keep us posted on how everything's going. Savannah's loving that swing; she's a far cry from the scared baby you found that day," Spartan observed, casting a glance at Savannah on the swing. "It's like everything fell perfectly into place for you and Charlie to have your baby."

"I count my blessings every day," I said.

"Didn't mean to make you tear up," Spartan chuckled.

"Thanks," I replied, grinning. "Any progress on that message?"

"Not yet. Charlie says it's all about a woman. But I can't think of any woman who loves me enough to cause a man to want me dead," Spartan said.

"What about Benni?" I suggested.

"Benni," he shook his head. "Benni doesn't love me; she hates me."

"Why does she hate you?" I inquired.

"Because the last time I saw her, we made love; I was furious because she was a virgin, and I stormed out of the room, slamming the door. I haven't seen her since then."

"Hold on, you slept with her, and left without saying anything?"

"No, I said something; it wasn't nice. I think I told her she needed to grow up and stop trying to make me love her because that would never happen," Spartan admitted.

"Fuck, that's harsh," I remarked.

"I know; I was angry because she seduced me into making love to her, and I didn't want her to be just another conquest that I fucked," Spartan confessed.

"But that's just what you made her into, by leaving. Just another conquest because you left the room and have ignored her since that day. Did you want her to be more than that?" I prodded.

"I don't know what I wanted," Spartan said, stepping off the porch.

"Liar!" I muttered under my breath.

"Did Spartan get another message?" Charlie asked, joining me.

"No, he was updating me on Adeline being in the hospital. The doctor doesn't seem optimistic, and his grandpa refuses to leave her side," I explained.

"Such a heartbreaking situation. Adeline once told me about how she reconnected with James Bellmont after all those years. It's sad that he has loved her all this time. I mean, what about the grandmother who didn't have his love? Do you think she knew he loved another woman?" Charlie pondered.

"I'm sure she felt loved. My grandma mentioned once told me that Spartan's grandmother was an unhappy woman and took it out on those around her," I replied.

"So she did know," Charlie nodded.

"Yeah, perhaps she did. I can imagine that would cause heartache, especially back then when people stayed in marriages regardless," I remarked.

"Mommy," Savannah's voice interrupted.

"I'll take over pushing; you take a break," I offered.

"Hey, I'm going to take you up on that."

Savannah squealed with delight as I pushed higher; she

was secured in her baby seat. Glancing at Charlie, I noticed her standing with her hands on her hips.

"Levi Bellmont, don't push her so high!" she called out.

I chuckled. "You heard Mommy, no swinging too high," I said, grinning. Yes, my life was indeed perfect.

THE END

Keep reading for a bonus epilogue about Steel and Charlie.

Ghost strolled over to where we were washing my truck, while Savannah happily wielded the hose, drenching Charlie and me just as thoroughly as herself. The sun beat down, but the refreshing spray kept us cool. "How are you holding up? We're truly sorry about Adeline. How is your grandpa doing?" I inquired.

"He seems alright, but I know Gramps. He's waiting for that time to come when he can be with her again. These last few years of his life are the happiest he's ever been. I'm grateful they had that time together," Ghost responded, watching us wash the truck.

Charlie approached, wrapping him in a hug. Adeline was a good person through and through. I'm glad she got to be with your grandpa. They had a powerful love, just like Steel and me and just like yours and Allison's. Don't you think it's time you did something before it's too late?" Charlie pressed, waiting for Ghost's response.

I think it might be already too late," Ghost replied, his voice heavy with resignation.

No, it's not too late yet. Go see her." Charlie urged.

"She's gone rock climbing with her brothers," Ghost said, walking over to sit on the steps.

"What? She climbs rocks? That sounds terrifying. I could never do that," Charlie remarked.

Both Ghost and I exchanged incredulous looks. "Sweetheart, you're a homicide detective. You've faced off with the cartel, taken down their top men, you've been kidnapped, shot, and had your vehicle flattened by a semi. Doctors said you would never walk again, but you proved them wrong. You've done far scarier things than climbing rocks," I pointed out.

"Yes, I know, but I wasn't hanging a thousand feet in the air, searching for a handhold," Charlie conceded.

"Are you afraid of heights?" I asked.

"Perhaps a little. I remember skiing with Marcus once. We were at the top of this massive mountain, and I was supposed to jump off the ski lift. I panicked. Marcus jumped, then turned to urge me on. He shouted for me to jump. And like an idiot, I jumped too late. I was maybe twenty feet from the ground, and I jumped," she picked up her cloth and continued to wash the truck.

"Don't leave us hanging," Ghost prompted.

"What happened next," I asked, waiting to hear her story.

She turned and looked at us. "When I hit the snow, I careened down that mountain uncontrollably, screaming so loudly it could've triggered an avalanche. At least, that's what Marcus claimed when we were at the bottom. I swear I nearly wet myself; I was so scared," Charlie confessed, prompting laughter from Ghost and me.

"How old were you then," I wondered, imagining her as a young teenager.

I was twenty-seven, and it was my second time skiing. I might've fibbed to Marcus, boasting about my skiing skills. I told him to watch out or I'd run him over. Well, I did. I zoomed past him so fast that my ski clipped his, sending him face-first into the snow," she recounted, chuckling along with us.

"I wish I could've seen that," Ghost said. I can't imagine you screaming.

Charlie and I exchanged glances, recalling her earlier morning scream when she was orgasming this morning.

"Trust me, it was terrifying. The rest of that weekend, everyone chuckled when they saw us," Charlie reminisced.

~

TWO MONTHS after Adeline's passing, Ghost's grandfather also passed away. His family surrounded him as he bid his final farewells. His funeral was held on Saturday, a day preceding the family reunion. While the family busied themselves with preparations, I found myself searching for Charlie.

"Has anyone seen Charlie?" I inquired.

"She's resting with Savannah," Sherry Scott said.

The Scotts came to every family gathering because they are part of our family now. I frowned because this was not the first time Charlie had fallen asleep during the day. I walked to Savannah's bedroom, and there they were both sleeping. *She did get up at four this morning, I was worried over nothing.* Reluctantly, I gently roused her; dinner was nearly served, and her presence was expected.

Running my hand along her side, Charlie stirred. "Hey, I'm sorry I fell asleep. What time is it?" she mumbled, blinking awake.

"You've only been asleep for a little while. Dinner is almost ready, and I know you'd want to be there when we start serving everyone."

"Thanks for waking me," she replied, rubbing her eyes.

"Sweetheart, are you sick?"

"No, I'm not sick, just tired. I went to bed at midnight and woke up at four. I'm fine; wipe that worried look off your face."

Looking at my wife, I was so grateful that she was mine, she was beautiful inside and out. Her long dark hair was braided and hung over her shoulder, and her brown eyes sparkled as she glanced down at Savannah. Taking her hand, I drew her close, planting a kiss on her lips.

"I love you so much. Have I told you that lately?" I whispered.

"Yes, earlier this morning. I love you, too. I'm not sick, just exhausted, I promise," she reassured me.

I believe you. Let's go have dinner," I said, smiling as we both glanced down to see Savannah stirring.

"Me hungry," Savannah announced. Savannah was sitting up, rubbing her eyes. I scooped her up, and we walked out to our guests.

As we stepped outside, the atmosphere turned tense. Benni stood there, radiating anger. But damn, she was hot. I looked at Charlie.

"Benni hasn't changed a bit; still the most beautiful woman around. Wonder what's got her worked up," I murmured.

"I don't know. Let me hand Savannah to Sherry, and we'll find out," I said, handing the baby to Grandma Sherry.

"What's wrong," I asked Spartan, who was gazing at Benni as if he was questioning his sanity for pushing her away.

This is what's wrong," Benni said, holding out a piece of paper.

Charlie accepted the paper cautiously, holding it by the corners, a scrap of brown paper bag with crayon writing on it. Charlie looked at me. "It says that if she or Amy dies, it'll be Levi Bellmont's fault because he refuses to die."

"Fuck," Spartan muttered, taking Benni's hand and leading her away from the others. Charlie and I followed.

"Let go of me," Benni growled.

"If I may interject, I can clarify things for Benni. Hello, Benni. I'm sure you don't remember me; I'm Charlie," Charlie introduced herself.

"Of course, I remember you, Charlie. I'm sorry I haven't been here to welcome you back to the Mountain."

"I know you are a busy woman, I read your digital newspaper when it comes out every week. What is going on is this: someone has been trying to get Spartan killed, and he received the same kind of letter as this one. He said it's your fault if she dies. So, in Spartan's letter, the person must have been talking about you, and who is Amy?" Charlie explained.

"Amy is my child, and if anyone ever gets anywhere near my daughter, I will kill them. I carry a gun, and I'm not afraid to use it. What's going on?" Benni demanded, turning to Spartan.

Spartan's expression shifted, clearly shaken by the revelation about Amy. "We don't know who's behind this, but now that you're involved, I'll ensure your safety, and your daughter's," he promised.

"Are you out of your mind? There's no way in hell I'm letting you guard me and my daughter. I'll hire my own protection."

"Alright, our team will guard both of you. Rebel and

Reaper will stay with you and your daughter, but you have to stay here on the mountain," Spartan insisted.

"You can't tell me what to do, Levi. I haven't taken orders from anyone since I was seventeen, and I won't start now. I'll handle this," Benni declared firmly.

"No, if you don't want this lunatic to harm you or your baby, you'll follow my instructions. This guy knows what he's doing. If he wants to hurt someone, he will, and since it's you he's after, he might target your daughter. You'll have to stay at the main house with my brothers. They'll keep you safe. Where's your daughter?" Spartan asked.

"She's at home with my brothers. This doesn't feel right, and I don't want to stay on this mountain. It's bad enough dodging you when visiting friends and family," Benni protested.

"You won't even know I'm around," Spartan said.

"I doubt we won't know you are around. Just stay away from me. I'll pack some things and drive over there tonight," Benni decided.

I saw Spartan shake his head. "I'll come with you and take you and your daughter to them. But first I need to make a call."

"Fine. I'm getting a plate of food," Benni said, turning away and saying hello to everyone.

"I think that went pretty well," Charlie said, smiling at Spartan.

"We'll see," Spartan replied cautiously.

"Let's get something to eat," I suggested, taking Charlie's hand.

"I don't want much. My stomach was upset this morning, but I'm not sick. Just not that very hungry, I've been snacking all day," Charlie explained.

"Alright, just a little then. I was worried about you," I

admitted, deciding to keep an eye on her myself to ascertain her condition.

The party was winding down, and our guest began to depart. I caught sight of Charlie at the swing set. My heart skipped a beat as she collapsed to the ground. Rushing to her side, I scooped her up.

"Sweetheart, what's wrong?" I asked, glancing around to see if Allison was nearby.

"Steel, please stop worrying; I was just exhausted. Put me down. You've got Grandma all worked up," she said as Grandma hurried over to us. "Grandma, I'm fine, just a bit dizzy, that's all. Steel, put me down."

"Allison, can you please check out Charlie for me? She's sick and won't tell me what's wrong with her."

"Stop, Steel, look at me. There is nothing wrong with me. I'm just a little tired. Quit letting your mind go wild with images of me being sick. I'm fine."

Allison rushed over. "Put her down, Steel; I'll take a look at her," I sat her down, and Allison and Bailey walked with her into the house.

"I'm alright just exhausted. Steel is worried because I've been so busy, and I've taken to napping lately," Bailey and Allison were both looked at me eagerly. "Why are you two looking at me like that?" I inquired.

"Charlie, we want you to take this pregnancy test just to clear the obvious up, and we'll know that's not why you are tired and dizzy. Didn't you mention you been sick a few times a couple of months ago."

"I'm not pregnant. I can't have children; we all know that."

"No, we don't," Allison interjected. "You mentioned your doctor's opinion, but what does he really know? Just take the test," she pleaded.

"Why do you have a pregnancy test on you?" I asked, perching on the bed.

"I've had it with me for a while," Bailey confessed, "I thought you might need it. I've had a hunch for some time."

"Bailey, I'm scared to take this test," I admitted trembling. I reached my hand out, took the test, and retreated to the bathroom. I took the test and walked back into my room, where Allison and Bailey were waiting. We sat in silence before Bailey checked her watch. We all headed to the bathroom together. All three of us looked at the test, and I fainted. When I came to Steel was carrying me to bed as Bailey and Allison left the room.

"Tell me what's wrong," Steel said.

I started crying. "Steel, we are pregnant."

"What did you say? Are we having a baby?"

"Yes, we're pregnant. That's why I've been sick and exhausted," I confessed. We turned as Savannah ran into the room, giggling. I lifted her up and held her close, before sitting back down beside Steel.

"Hey, sweetheart, do you want a baby brother or sister?" I asked as Steel wrapped his arms around us.

"Sister," Savannah exclaimed, and we chuckled.

"We are going to have a baby," Steel murmured, shaking his head.

"Are you sure everything will be okay? The doctor said you couldn't have babies. What if something goes wrong?"

"Nothing will go wrong. The doctor thought I couldn't conceive because of the accident. He thought I wouldn't get pregnant. But he was mistaken, and I'm pregnant. In fact, the more I think about it... wait a moment. I'm four months along. We are having a baby in five months. We have so much to do before the baby arrives."

"Sweetheart, the first thing we're doing is seeing the

doctor tomorrow. We need to ensure your health isn't at risk," Steel insisted.

"I'm fine, you'll see. Let's tell everyone that Savannah will be a big sister in five months. I feel like crying," I said as tears welled up. "But let's not go out just yet. I need a moment."

"Sweetheart," Steel said, wiping his eyes. "I want to talk to Allison. What did she have to say about the baby?"

"She said I should call that doctor back and tell him to kiss my ass!"

"She didn't say that," he replied incredulously.

"You're right," I admitted, "she said something worse, but I didn't want to say it in front of Savannah."

He chuckled. "So, we are having a baby."

"Yes, we are having a baby."

Dearest reader.

Thank you, for your continued support. I really appreciate that you read my books.

If you can please leave me a review for this book, I would appreciate it enormously.

Your reviews allow me to get validation I need to keep going as an Indie author.

Just a moment of your time is all that is needed. I will try my best to give you the

best books I can write.

Keep reading for more Delta Force Guardians. Ghost and Allison's story. Expect lot's of Action and Adventure, plus a lot of steam; after all they have to stop and make up each time they fight.

Ghost My Book

30

GHOST

As I glanced at my sister Carrie, tears welled in her eyes as we packed up Gramp's room. If she didn't stop, I'd need to fetch another box of tissues. We were all dealing with the loss of our grandfather in our own way. We were all going to miss him, he raised Carrie, me and our cousins after our parent's died in an accident.

"Look what I found," Carrie exclaimed for the umpteenth time. Grandpa had saved everything we kids had ever made for him. Spartan walked in, took a seat on the bed, and ran his fingers through his hair.

"I can't wrap my head around the fact that he's gone," he murmured, wiping his sleeve across his face. "We're like orphans now."

I heard Carrie chuckle, and then I sat down and chuckled. "You should see the stuff he's kept. Everything we ever made for him is tucked away in boxes in the closet."

This was the first time Spartan had been here since Rebel and Reaper brought Benni and her daughter Amy to stay here due to a threat on their lives. While I knew they had a shared history, I didn't pry; my own tangled history, with Allison Reed left me without much room to give advice on matters of the heart.

A week had passed since our grandfather's passing, and the weight of it hung heavy on all of us. Steel entered, searching for us. "I heard something from Jacob," he said, referring to his brother. "He says the Russian Mafia is prowling around our area, looking for someone."

"The Russian Mafia usually keeps to themselves. Who could they be after around here?" I asked.

"Marcus will be here any minute to brief us on the situation. Even though he mostly worked with the Mexican cartel, his friend passed along some intel on these guys, just in case they show up here," Spartan explained.

"How's Marcus adjusting without all that excitement he's used to?" I inquired.

"He's loving it. He gets plenty of excitement with my sister Jaz and the kids. I don't believe we have to worry about the Russian Mafia. I think that's Marcus. Did you want to hear what he has to say?" Spartan asked.

"Yeah, I'll be right down," I turned to my sister, Carrie, "why don't you take a break? We'll do more tomorrow."

"Okay, I should get home. I'll see you tomorrow."

I made my way downstairs to the kitchen, our usual gathering spot. Marcus leaned against the counter. "Here's what I found out: the guy they're after is a hitman who shot one of their leaders. He's injured, so he can't have gotten far. Last they traced him, he was in this area," Marcus said.

"So, he's wounded and hiding out nearby. Should we inform the people around here that an injured Russian Mafia might be in this area?" I suggested.

"Yeah, probably a good idea. Hopefully, he's already moved on," Marcus said.

"Why do they suspect he's around here?" I asked, turning to Marcus.

"They found his car not far from here. It ran out of gas, and they saw blood beside it," Marcus replied.

"Do you think he might be in someone's house?" I frowned.

Just then, Viper's phone rang. "Hey, Allison, what's up?

"Viper, there are armed men in the hospital, threatening to shoot people if we don't hand over someone to them.. They said they are going to start shooting people if we don't hand someone over to them."

"I'm putting you on speaker," Viper said, then turned to us.

"I can't talk long. I'm hiding in the nurse's station with some patients," Allison whispered, sounding scared.

That's all I needed to hear. I bolted out the door and into my vehicle within seconds. I was getting her out of that hospital, even if it meant killing the Russian Mafia single-handedly.

Before I could put my car into gear, Viper and Spartan jumped into my car. "You need to calm down, Ghost. You'll be no good to Allison if you charge in like a madman. Spartan chided. "Running in there recklessly will only get you shot."

He was right, and I knew it. I took a deep breath, attempting to steady my pounding heart. Do you think the entire police force is there?" I asked.

"Jacob mentioned they were. Getting close will be tough," Viper replied.

"I'll park a couple of blocks away and sneak into the hospital. We need to find out which floor Allison's on so we can get her out and deal with those Russian Mafia scum. Do you think the hospital is hiding the other guy?" I glanced at the others.

"I'll call Ryan or one of my other brothers knows what floor Allison's on," Viper offered. "We can't let them know what's happening, or they'll be down here."

We made it to the city in record time, and I parked two blocks away with our weapons on us; we cut our way through trees until we reached the hospital and looked at each other. Every police car in the county must have been there.

Viper's phone buzzed, and he looked at it. Ryan had texted that Allison worked on the third floor. It was the cardiac floor. "Why don't we each take a floor since we don't know what floor the Russians are on? If they are shooting, we'll probably hear them," I said, glancing at the guys.

"I'll take the third floor to where Allison is," Viper said. "That way she won't blow her top when she sees you, and the two of you won't start arguing."

"Really, Viper, do I look like an idiot? I'm getting Allison out of that hospital if I have to carry her kicking and screaming from there," and another thing, "How the hell would I argue with her when she won't even talk to me?" Ghost said angrily.

"Okay, you go to the third floor. Just remember Allison is our only sister, and we want her to live a long life," I wasn't even going to answer that question; Viper knew how much I loved Allison. We made our way to the side of the hospital.

I looked up and saw a ladder high up on the wall. I looked at Viper. He held his hands together. I put my foot in it, and he pushed me up into the air. My fingers almost touched the ladder one more time, and I grabbed the ladder.

We lifted and pulled each other up until all of us were on the ladder.

Fuck, we saw three police officers run around the building. When they looked up, I put my fingers to my lips. I was surprised when they nodded and kept going.

Viper jumped on the rooftop of the second floor. I kept going up until I reached the rooftop of the third floor. Hopefully, they had an open window so I could get inside.

31

ALLISON

I could hear the voices of those men; their Russian language made their identity clear. The sound of a woman's screams pierced the air; I couldn't stay in here knowing someone needed my help. Glancing at the nurse and the four patients we had managed to get into the break room, I felt a surge of determination.

"Stay put; I'm going to go out there and see who needs my help," I declared, my voice quivering as I made my way to the door, I couldn't stay hidden when someone needed help.

The bastard was trying to rape Sandy, one of the nurses on the floor. She was also Steel's cousin. Instinctively I grabbed an object from the nurse's station and hit him on the head, but it didn't seem to bother him.

He remained unfazed, towering over me, I was used to men who towered over me. all of my brothers were huge. This guy wasn't as imposing as Ghost. There I go again, measuring every man I saw to Ghost. Now, I probably would never see him again because I was pretty sure I was about to die.

The man wrapped his hand around my throat and picked me up in the air; his grip tightened around my throat. My hands swung to hit him, and then Sandy jumped on his back, and he threw her off.

Blinking to clear my vision, I caught a glimpse of Ghost through the window; his expression contorted with rage. The shattering of glass accompanied his arrival, and as I was thrown against the wall, Ghost powerful fist connected with the Russian's face.

I helped Sandy up off the floor; she remained shaken and tearful, urging her to seek refuge along with the others. Sandy, lock yourself in the nurse's breakroom with the others. Is there anyone else here?"

Yes, they're in the radiology room. Come with me," Sandy replied, her voice trembling.

"No, I'm going to help Ghost," I insisted, pushing her toward the break room. He might not need my help, but I wasn't going to take any chances that man had a knife or gun.

Despite our estrangement, my feelings for Ghost remained unchanged; the memory of discovering him in bed with another woman was still fresh in my mind, even though it was five years ago, extinguishing any hope of reconciliation.

Ghost, whose real name is James Belmont, earned his name in the Delta Force Team. His sister Carrie, my closest friend, served as an unspoken link between us. The pain of our shattered engagement, five years past, lingered, compelling me to leave the mountain where Ghost lived. While I missed my home and family, the anguish of seeing Ghost daily had become unbearable. I yearned for a love that would love me as I deserved.

He strayed, and I wasn't forgiving him. They both woke

up when I screamed, with the woman running off naked and Ghost pretending not to know how that woman ended up in his bed.

I saw the Russian reach for his boot and saw the gun; before I could intervene, I heard the sickening sound of the man's neck snapping. Ghost stood up and looked at me.

That's when we heard boots running. I quickly wondered how they got in when we had the floor locked down and the doors locked. "Run," Ghost whispered as he ran toward whoever wore those heavy-sounding boots. I grabbed the gun from the dead man's boot and followed quietly. I saw two men laugh when Ghost stopped and smiled at them.

Doesn't he realize he's pissing them off? They came at him at the same time, and I watched as he kicked their ass. They fought for what seemed like forever; when I saw one of the guys reach for his boot, I knew there was a gun, and I was right. He was going to kill Ghost; I didn't think I didn't have time.

I didn't see the gun in Ghost's hand; I only saw the gun pointed at him and the man smiling. I fired the gun I had and shot the man. I hit his arm, and I heard Ghost shout before the man turned and shot me four times.

I don't know what happened after that, and I didn't hear Ghost screaming for help or Viper crying as he tried to save my life.

Everything blurred as I looked around at my departed loved ones. Embraced by pure joy, I saw the radiant essence of everyones souls, illuminated like stars; the feeling was so wonderful I only felt happiness. Suddenly, the cries of Viper and Ghost shattered the serenity, dragging me back to agonizing consciousness; my body wracked with pain as I drew breath once more.

32

GHOST

I cradled Allison's face in my hands, pressing a gentle kiss to her soft lips, giving her breath before I sprung into action to help Viper save her life. Once she could breathe, she was rushed down to surgery, and I looked at Viper.

"How did this happen?" Viper demanded. "You promised to keep her safe, so I want you to tell me how my sister ended up getting shot four times before I kill you."

"I don't know," I replied, anguish surging through my body. Rising to my feet, I followed the gurney that rushed to take Allison to the operating room.

Viper was right next to me. "Explain to me what the hell went wrong?" he demanded.

"I killed the first guy, and then these two showed up. I told Allison to run to safety where the others were. She fucking didn't listen to me; I thought she had followed my orders until one of them pulled out his gun," I took a shaky breath and continued talking.

"When the bastard pulled the gun out, I heard another gun go off, and the man turned so fast and started shooting.

I shot them both, which was what I was about to do before Allison fired her shot. It was too late," I explained.

"Where did she get the fucking gun?" Viper demanded.

"The first Russian had it in his boot. She must have grabbed it when I went after the other two. She followed me; I should have watched and ensured she left."

"You didn't have time to ensure she had done what you told her to do. Allison would never leave you to take care of those men yourself. She loves you too damn much," Viper frowned, glancing over at me.

"This has gone on for six fucking years, and you need to fix this when she wakes up. Either the two of you are together, or you are apart. You can't have it both ways any longer. My sister wants a family, and if she will never forgive you, then I want you to make sure she knows it's time to move on. I want you tell her when she's better that it's over, tell her if she can't forgive you then you don't want to be with her."

"I haven't done anything to be forgiven for, and you damn well know it! Allison is the only one who doubts that. If she trusted me as she should, she would know I'd never cheat on her. She knows how much I love her. I would never do that, and I'm tired of defending myself for something I didn't do," Ghost declared before walking away.

"Where are you going?" Viper asked, puzzled.

"To the operating room. I'll make sure nothing happens to Allison during surgery."

They won't let you in. Let's wait in the waiting room. My brothers will be here soon," Viper suggested.

"How would your brothers be here soon? We haven't called them," I said.

"No, but I'm sure Jacob did," Viper explained.

"Yeah, I forgot Jacob was there; I'm sure the whole

mountain knows about it by now. Why don't you come with me to the surgery room? At least you'll know what is going on instead of being in the waiting room not knowing anything," I said. That's when I looked at Viper and then down at myself. The both of us were covered in Allison's blood.

I leaned against the wall before I slid down; Viper slid down next to me, and I glanced over at him. "I can't think about her losing all this blood; I can't lose her. I know we aren't together. But I know where she is. When she comes out of this we are going to sit down and talk, if I have to tie her down. She had to know that I would never cheat on her, no matter how drunk I was," I said.

"She has it all warped inside her head, letting her thoughts take over and grow out of control. No telling what all she's let her mind imagine," Viper explained. Why don't we shower and change our clothes?

"I'm going to call Bailey and have her bring me something to wear, and I'll shower here. Do you want me to have her bring you something?" Viper asked.

"She can have Izzy watch the kids, so she won't have to worry about them," he said looking down at his clothes he wiped his sleeve across his eyes and walked away.

I put on a hospital gown and walked into the surgery room. I stood against the back wall as they operated on Allison, and then things changed. I saw panic in the nurse's eyes as she looked at me, and I realized it was Sammy, my cousin.

I didn't care what they said to me; I walked over, took Allison's hand, and begged her to live. "Sweetheart, please fight to stay here with me. I don't want to be on this earth if you aren't here. I love you so much. Please don't leave me."

The doctor continued his frantic work while I whispered in her ear how much I loved her. I heard a sigh like everyone had been holding their breath, and I looked at Allison, who was once again breathing.

"Get him out of here, Levi, leave," Gordan Cantrell said, not taking his eyes off Allison. I was surprised he remembered me. I hadn't seen him since high school. I glanced his way and remembered Sammy saying he was a surgeon.

"Save her," I said before leaving the room. I sat in the waiting room with everyone. I had on clean clothes. I didn't join in on any conversation with my family or Allison's family. All I could concentrate on was Allison in that surgery room.

After four hours, I got up and headed back to the operating room. Viper and his brothers followed me. We waited outside of the room another hour before the doctor came out and looked at us.

"She's still alive. The surgery is over; now we all pray for the next forty-eight hours. That's when we will know if she's going to live. They'll take her to the intensive care unit; she can have two visitors at a time, no more than that."

I didn't like the sound of that. He didn't say she would be alright. "Wait, is she going to be alright?" I asked, stepping around the others to get closer to him.

"Gordon said we need another forty-eight hours before we know if Allison will live. You and the Delta Force Team know more than most what a bullet can do to your body. Plus, she hit her head, so there are a lot of injuries Allison has to overcome."

Join me on social media Follow me on BookBub
https://www.bookbub.com/profile/susie-mciver

. . .

Newsletter Sign Up http://bit.ly/SusieMcIver_Newsletter

Facebook Group:
https://www.facebook.com/SusieMcIverAuthor

https://www.susiemciver.com/

https://www.instagram.com/susiemciverauthor/
https://www.susiemciver.com/

Printed in Great Britain
by Amazon